TORCHWOOD

SOMETHING
IN THE WATER

The *Torchwood* series from BBC Books:

TORCHWOOD
SOMETHING
IN THE WATER

Trevor Baxendale

2 4 6 8 10 9 7 5 3 1

Published in 2008 by BBC Books, an imprint of Ebury Publishing
A Random House Group company
Torchwood is a BBC Wales production for BBC Two
Executive Producers: Russell T Davies and Julie Gardner
Co-producer: Chris Chibnall
Series Producer: Richard Stokes
The Random House Group Limited Reg. No. 954009.
Addresses for companies within the Random House Group can be found at
www.randomhouse.co.uk.

A CIP catalogue record for this book is available from the British Library.

ISBN 978 1 84607 437 0

The Random House Group Limited supports The Forest Stewardship Council
(FSC), the leading international forest certification organisation. All our titles
that are printed on Greenpeace approved FSC certified paper carry the FSC
logo. Our paper procurement policy can be found at www.rbooks.co.uk/
environment

Commissioning Editor: Albert DePetrillo
Series Editor: Steve Tribe
Production Controller: Phil Spencer

Cover design by Lee Binding @ Tea Lady © BBC 2008
Typeset in Albertina and Century Gothic
Printed and bound in Germany by GGP Media GmbH, Poessneck

For Martine, Luke and Konnie – with love, as always

The late Bob Strong. That's what they called him.

He'd been late all his life. Late for school, late for university lectures, late for dates. He'd even managed to be late when he was on a promise with Nurse Carrick, the lovely, gorgeous, drop-dead sexy Lucy Carrick. One flat tyre had robbed him of the night of his life and ever since then his hot and lustful affair with Juicy Lucy had been conducted entirely in his own imagination.

And so now here he was, late for surgery (again) and still lost in idle fantasies about Lucy.

He scrambled out of the car, grabbed his briefcase, then ran in through the sliding doors of the Trynsel Medical Centre. The waiting room, he noted with dismay, was already full of people coughing. Coughing quite badly, actually. Lots of tissues held to mouths and that curious, ripe smell of bacteria-rich mucus membranes. 'It's going to be a long day,' he thought. 'Just as well, with me being this late.'

'Morning Dr Bob,' called Letitia Bird, the receptionist. She was smiling, but it was a cruel smile. She enjoyed nothing more than seeing Bob arrive late and flustered. She'd had plenty of opportunities. Bob knew Letty fancied Trynsel's senior doctor and practice manager, Iuean Davis, and held all the other GPs in complete contempt. That raised them only one level up from the rest of humanity, which she held in complete and utter contempt.

'Slept in again?' Letty asked pointedly.

'Of course not.' Bob tried to flatten down the sticky-up hair on the back of his head. 'It was the traffic. Backed right the way up the Caerphilly Road.'

Letty's reply was little more than a slight pursing of her razor-thin lips. *If you say so.*

'Ah! There he is,' boomed a familiar Welsh baritone. 'The luckiest bloody Englishman in Wales!'

Bob turned to see Iuean Davis approaching with an envelope. 'In my hand I have a piece of paper…' he began, and then laughed. 'Actually, two pieces. Tickets to the RBS Six Nations match between England and Wales, no less. That's one for you… and one for me, if my powers of mathematics haven't bloody well deserted me.'

Bob stopped in his tracks, genuinely touched. 'Iuean, that's fantastic… Gosh, how much do I owe you?'

'Nothing! My treat. Actually I got them free from an old college mate, but I'm not telling you that. And anyway, there's always a down side, mind: it's at the Millennium Stadium, so if the English beat us I will charge you for the ticket, and the bloody bus fare to boot.'

Bob grinned, clapped Iuean on the shoulder and thanked him again. 'Look, I'll catch you later, Iuean. I'm running a bit behind schedule.'

'Fashionably late, Bob, fashionably late…' Iuean swept imperiously by, waving the tickets in the air.

Bob collapsed into his surgery room and shut the door behind him. Then he threw his briefcase down on the floor by his desk and slumped into his chair. He sat for a minute and tried to get his breath back. He was feeling pretty grim this morning, he had to admit. He hadn't drunk all that much the night before, so he hoped he wasn't coming down with something. Come to think of it, he could feel the start of a sore throat developing.

Bob switched his laptop on and waited for it to request a password. His first patient was due in – he checked his watch – minus five minutes. Damn.

The intercom buzzed. 'Are you ready for Miss Harden, Dr Bob?' asked Letty with pointed innocence.

Saskia Harden! Bob felt his pulse quicken and his face start to blush. What the hell was she doing here? Quickly he brought up his diary on the laptop. Bloody hellfire! How could he have forgotten she was coming in this morning? Too much time thinking about Juicy Lucy Carrick, that's how.

'Yes, of course,' Bob lied. 'Send her right in.'

He tried to calm his hair down again – it seemed to be spring-loaded this morning – and then neatened up the papers and pens on his desk as best he could. One of the pens slipped out from beneath his fingers, skidded across the desk and rolled onto the floor. Bob leapt out of his seat, intending to circle the desk to retrieve it. But he tripped over his briefcase and stumbled sideways just as the door started to open.

Trying to save the situation, Bob converted his fall into an attempt to look as though he was leaning nonchalantly on his desk, but the angle of his body was way too steep. At forty-five degrees, one hand on the desk and the other on his hip, he looked absurd. And he knew it.

'Hello, good morning, come in,' he trilled to the creature that stepped into his surgery.

Saskia Harden was no beauty, but she had the kind of looks that turned people's heads. Men and women. The fact that she had tried to kill herself on a number of occasions only added to the air of exotic mystery that had built up around her at Trynsel, and had led Iuean Davis to christen her 'the Angel of Death'.

She was always cool, almost statuesque, with a face that looked as if it had been carved from some sort of smooth, living stone. Her eyes were smoky, amused, scornful, hopeful, all at once, as if she was somehow physically removed from everything and everyone else, acting only as an impartial observer.

Letty Bird had once described her as 'that woman who always looks like she's on the other side of a pane of glass'.

Saskia walked into the surgery and closed the door softly behind her. She was wearing a thin, light raincoat belted at the waist. Her legs were bare below the knee, apart from her shoes, and this gave the impression that she wasn't wearing anything beneath the coat. Bob felt his pulse quickening.

'Is this yours?' she asked, bending neatly to pick up Bob's pen.

'Thanks, yeah.' Bob straightened awkwardly, took the pen, tossed it carelessly onto his desk and watched it roll off the other side and drop onto the carpet again. 'Look at me – all fingers and thumbs this morning.' He laughed and sat down, indicating that she should take a seat as well.

Saskia Harden slid demurely into the patient's chair opposite and smiled at him. She had the strangest smile but it was her eyes that captivated him. They seemed distant and yet extraordinarily focused, as if they could see things that no one else could.

Bob thought of them as the eyes of a predator, sizing up its prey from deep cover.

It was also hard to describe exactly what colour they were. It was almost too easy to say they were green, and not strictly accurate. Not quite green, then. Grey? Not really. Jade? No. Emerald? Absolutely not. Somewhere in between, perhaps. All of them and none of them, depending on the light and the time of day, whether she was indoors or outdoors, morning or afternoon or midnight. Her eyes had that kind of variable quality, what jewellers refer to as *chatoyance*. Bob even wondered if she used tinted contact lenses.

Suddenly realising that he had been staring deeply into her eyes for far too long as he tried to make sure, he found her smiling that smile at him again. The smile that made him think she either wanted to kiss him or kill him.

'Right!' he said, clearing his throat and sitting back. He put his hands behind his head in an effort to look relaxed, but then, worried there might already be sweat-patches under his arms, sat forward and folded them on the desk instead. 'What can we do for you this morning? I mean, what can I do for you this morning? Anything?'

'I've come back for my check-up,' she replied, still smiling.

'Of course.' Bob turned to his laptop and quickly accessed her records. 'Right, let's see.' He looked back up at her. 'How's it going? How are you feeling?'

'Fantastic.'

Bob raised his eyebrows. 'Good. Great! So – as I said. What can I do for you?'

She leaned forward, keeping his gaze. Her liquid, not-green not-grey eyes were mesmerising. 'Dr Strong, I'll be blunt: I need to find a man.' When she spoke next, her voice was little more than a dark whisper. 'I want to procreate.'

'I see,' said Bob, equally quietly, and then cleared his throat again. This time it was difficult, like there was a real cough there.

'I think you can help me with that, Dr Strong.'

'What? No, I don't think so. I mean no. No. Well, not me personally, if you understand. What I mean is…'

He was blithering. Doing exactly what Iuean always complained about.

But Saskia seemed not to notice, or perhaps care. She said, 'I'm looking for the right kind of man. And I think you're the one.'

'Ah,' he said, for want of anything more intelligent to say. He decided at this point it was best to just shut his mouth and say as little as possible. At least until his brain starting thinking again. Saskia was staring back at him, and he had a sudden vision of himself lying on top of her, looking down into those indefinable green-grey eyes as he made love to her on his desk.

Bob shook his head to clear it. 'Saskia – Miss Harden – you've been coming to see me every week for the last month. I know you've had your problems with the police, and I have agreed to help and support you in your recovery as much as I can but…' He struggled for something to say and then opted for a weak smile. 'I have to draw the line somewhere.'

She looked away from him for the first time, and Bob felt

as though a light had been turned off somewhere. The world was suddenly a dimmer place. He coughed politely to make her look up at him again. 'I'm sorry, I don't mean to sound rude. It's just that…'

'What?'

He couldn't see what she was wearing under the raincoat – there was only a triangle of pale flesh visible between the lapels. There really was nothing to suggest that she was wearing anything at all underneath. He wondered what it would be like to kiss those strange, mysterious lips.

Bob coughed again and sat back in his chair, taking in a good breath of air. Finally, finally, his professional training reasserted itself. 'OK,' he said. 'Saskia. Don't get me wrong. But this isn't the time or the place for… for this. It's not that I'm not interested. But I am a doctor. There are rules about this sort of thing.'

'Rules?'

'Yeah.' He sat forward and punched some keys on the laptop, making sure that he didn't look into her eyes again. 'Look. You show every sign of making a full and proper recovery – but I want to keep things professional. I have to keep things professional. At least in this surgery. You must understand that. OK?'

She didn't say anything, but she didn't need to. Her eyes told him everything he needed to know: that what he had said made no difference to her at all. His words had been no more than the pathetic bleating of a lamb under the watchful eyes of the wolf. Eyes that were still full of hunger, a strange, inexplicable craving that went beyond simple lust. Bob found he was completely unable to speak or move. In that timeless interval in the conversation, Bob was suddenly and coldly struck by how appropriate the name Angel of Death was for her.

Because, somewhere deep inside him, he realised that he was absolutely terrified of this woman.

The eyes blinked, as cool and grey as an alligator gliding under the water's surface. 'Well then,' she said, unfolding herself from the seat. 'I'd better be going. Catch you another time.'

Bob stood up awkwardly, aware that he was sweating. He tried smiling at her and held a hand towards the door. 'I'll set up another appointment for you next week,' he told her. 'See Miss Bird on the desk on the way out and she'll confirm the time. OK?'

She nodded and left. Bob stood in the doorway for a few moments and watched her walk away, his eyes fixed on the sway of her hips beneath the material of her raincoat. He felt nothing. The attraction had simply vanished, leaving a freezing ache in his chest and throat.

When he lifted his hands to his face, they were visibly shaking.

ONE

Owen Harper was waiting on the street corner, pulling his leather jacket tighter to keep out the worst of the drizzle. A cold wind blew in from the River Taff, dragging a squall of freezing rain through the grey city streets. It was bad weather, even for a late-summer night in Cardiff, and Owen hated waiting at the best of times.

He checked his watch, angling his wrist towards the nearest street light so that he could see the display. At exactly two minutes to midnight, he heard the growl of an engine and then a big black off-roader appeared around the corner, blue lights flickering in the windscreen. The SUV skidded to a halt right next to him, TORCHWOOD stencilled in black on the rain-speckled wing.

The passenger door popped open, and Owen peered inside. 'Going my way?' he asked with more than a hint of sarcasm.

The interior was illuminated by a complicated range of VDUs and dashboard controls. Captain Jack Harkness was at the wheel, a broad grin on his face. 'All the way,' he said.

'I bet you pick up guys like this all the time,' said Owen as he climbed in and shut the door.

'It's the car,' Jack smiled. 'Everyone digs the car.'

The SUV surged forward. 'So, where are you taking me tonight?' Owen inquired politely. 'Dinner? Pictures? Underground car park?'

'It's a surprise.'

A chain-link fence flashed by, topped by old plastic bags caught on the barbed wire and fluttering in the wind.

'Charming spot,' Owen remarked.

'Industrial estate,' said Jack. 'Weevil country.'

This got Owen's full attention. 'You've seen him?'

'We've accessed CCTV security footage of the area from the cops. No doubt about it, Big Guy's here somewhere.'

Owen let out a whistle. Big Guy was a rogue Weevil that had been giving them the slip for nearly two months; it had left a trail of dead and injured throughout Butetown, always disappearing back into the sewer system before they could catch it.

'No wonder you dragged me out of bed.'

Jack glanced across at him. 'Well, you are our go-to guy for Weevils.'

'Yeah.' Owen felt the junction of his neck and shoulder a little nervously. He had suffered a bad Weevil bite not all that long ago and the wound still ached. 'Where are the others?'

'Ghost hunting near Newport.'

'Oh.' Owen wondered at this. It was unusual for just two of them to go after a Weevil; but then Big Guy was unusual. He didn't question the importance of ghost hunting in Newport compared to taking Big Guy down. Jack was wearing the kind of face that didn't welcome questions like that. Owen guessed that he knew the situation wasn't ideal but didn't want to miss a chance of catching the Weevil.

Jack slung the SUV around another corner and met a roadblock. The wet night air was full of flashing blue lights and policemen in large fluorescent jackets. He slowed down, negotiating a couple of squad cars until he drew level with one of the cops, a big sergeant with a bushy ginger moustache and watchful eyes. Jack slid the driver's window down and the sergeant leaned in, removing his cap first and shaking the rain off it.

'Evenin' all,' said Owen.

The sergeant glared at him but then flicked his gaze back to Jack, acknowledging his authority. 'Reckon we've got your man holed up in that warehouse,' the policeman said gravely. He used his cap to indicate a low, two-storey building further down the street. 'Standing orders are to leave these things to Torchwood – so this is me, leaving it to you, OK?'

'OK,' Jack nodded.

The policeman looked him up and down and Jack raised an eyebrow. 'Want my phone number, constable?'

'That's Sergeant Thomas, to you, sir,' replied the policeman solemnly. 'And no, I do not.'

He stepped back, waving them on, and Jack turned to Owen with a rueful smile. 'Can't win 'em all!'

Then he tooled the SUV past the cordon and they left the blue lights in a cloud of carbon-neutral exhaust.

'That's the place.' Jack slowed down and nodded at a crumbling sandstone building. It looked cold and forgotten, silhouetted against the dull orange furnace of the city beyond.

'It'll be deserted,' Owen said. 'The blues and twos will have scared it off.'

Jack shook his head. 'The cops have put men on all the sewer entrances within a half-mile radius. Big Guy's in there, and he's ours.'

Owen shifted in his seat so that he could reach the stungun in his jacket pocket.

'Leave it,' Jack advised. 'This guy's too big and he's going to be mad as a bagful of rattlesnakes. We'll never get close enough to be polite. This one's going down.'

He speeded up again as they approached the warehouse, the SUV's powerful halogens throwing up fat circles of light across a pair of wide doors. Owen saw some faded lettering over the entrance, but the SUV was now moving too fast for him to read it; Jack had floored the accelerator and the SUV was charging forward. The lights grew brighter as it approached the brick wall, and Owen flung up a hand to protect his face against the inevitable collision but, at the last second, Jack twisted the wheel again, slewed the car right around and hit the wooden doors broadside.

The SUV rocked under the impact but the doors gave, splintering as the old wood fell apart along seams of wet rot. The vehicle turned again, the heavy tyres losing their grip on the wet concrete floor of the warehouse, and the headlamps sent searchlight beams roving crazily around the darkened interior. They glimpsed metal pillars, stairs, balconies and a huge pile of bin bags in one corner.

Jack had his door open before the SUV had fully come to a halt, was out and running, gun in hand. His boots echoed across the hard floor, causing rats to flood out of the bin bags and into the shadows. Owen followed, drawing his own gun, hearing the triumphant shout as Jack saw something moving on the far side of the room.

'Up there!' Jack flicked on a powerful LED torch, its beam zigzagging up a metal staircase. 'Stop it!'

Owen snapped off a couple of shots in the right direction, but the rounds drew nothing more than sparks off metal. The boom of the heavy automatic reverberated around the warehouse like trapped thunder looking for a way out.

Without breaking his stride, Owen sprinted for the stairs leading up the gantry. Jack was right behind him, and he must have seen the thing again, because next Owen heard the heavy crack of Jack's old Webley revolver, and more sparks flew somewhere up in the darkness.

They split up, Owen taking the stairs on the left while Jack headed right. Owen took the metal steps three at a time, thighs straining, but he had to make the effort. They had been chasing this particular Weevil for long enough. It was big, tough and bastard cunning. Finally, they had it trapped.

Owen reached the landing and dropped to a crouch, arms extended, gun in both hands, trying not to breathe too hard. He didn't want to compromise his aim, for one thing, and then there was the smell.

'This place is bloody rank,' Owen said. 'What the hell's making that stench?'

Jack's reply came promptly from the shadows: 'Shh! Thought I saw something…'

Owen concentrated. The shadows were deep up here, and huge, grimy cobwebs floated among the girders of the ceiling and balcony like ghosts.

But there was something, up ahead, moving slowly in the darkness. Owen levelled his gun quickly, feeling a familiar surge of adrenalin. Then he forced himself to slow down; to do it properly. He summoned the clarity of mind he used on the shooting range and sighted carefully along the automatic's barrel, weapon held high, level with his eye.

He thought he could see it – just a silhouette, no more than one clot of darkness among all the others, but something was wrong. It didn't have the right shape for a Weevil. It didn't sound like one either – no harsh breathing or guttural noises.

The target spun, dropped, and Owen's shot went wide. Something clanged at the far end of the landing and he heard Jack shout. For a horrible moment Owen thought he'd hit him, but then he saw Jack running back down the stairs, greatcoat flapping behind him like bat wings.

Bloody hell! The thing had jumped. Straight off the gantry, a forty-foot drop.

Suicide, normally, even for a Weevil. But Torchwood didn't deal with normal.

Owen swore loudly and doubled back, hurrying down the steps.

He found Jack at the bottom, circling the area warily, gun held down in a two-handed grip. He didn't look happy.

'Don't tell me we lost it,' Owen said between breaths. 'Not after all this.'

'No way,' Jack snapped. 'It's in here somewhere and it's not leaving.'

For a second, all they could hear was their own heavy breathing. They stood still and listened carefully. The warehouse wasn't huge, but it was full of echoes and dark places. It would be possible to hide in here – but not for ever.

A rat darted out of a side opening and disappeared into

the shadows. Owen realised the significance immediately, exchanging a nod with Jack. Something had spooked that rat.

'This way,' said Jack quietly, moving forward, pistol raised.

Owen followed him through the narrow doorway into a tiled passage. There was just enough light to see their way through to a large chamber on the far side. It was cold in here and there was a sound – unmistakably water, gently lapping at the edges of a large tank. It sounded to Owen like they had wandered into a swimming baths.

'Phew! What is this place?' hissed Owen, scouring the gloom. The terrible stench of putrefying waste was far worse here, hitting them like a wall of offal.

'Fish farm. Used to be, anyway. Closed down and scheduled for demolition.'

'Can't come soon enough.'

'Hold it.' Jack stopped, held up a warning hand. He shone his torch down at his feet and found that he was standing in a large puddle of dark blood. Close by, a Weevil lay on its back, mouth open wide, stomach and chest opened even wider.

The rancid stench of Weevil blood hit Owen, and he clamped a hand over his mouth, gagging reflexively. 'God almighty,' he hissed a moment later, swallowing down the bile. 'What the hell did that to him?'

'It's Big Guy,' Jack said.

'Was Big Guy.' Owen, recovering, took a closer, more professional look. The bestial features were frozen in a surprised snarl. Fangs glinted in the torch light. Further down, torn muscle and intestines filled a gaping wound. 'He's been ripped open like a packet of crisps. Not many things could do that to a Weevil.'

They exchanged a look of mutual puzzlement, and then suddenly turned back to back, ignoring the corpse, covering each other.

'Whatever it was, it may still be here,' Jack whispered.

There was still water in the holding tanks. They were set in the floor, six feet deep, two rows of three. 'This used to be a public baths,' Jack said, confirming Owen's initial assessment. 'It was built early last century, converted into a fish farm in 1982. They split the swimming pool into six separate tanks to keep the fish in.'

Owen had his torch out now, the beam chasing across the calcified tiles and into the rectangles of black water.

'Stagnant,' he said. Green algae filmed the still surface of the nearest pool, crawling up the sides of the tanks and between the cracks in the tiles. 'No wonder it stinks so much in here. Weevils are bad enough at the best of times, but this place is something else.'

Jack was circling around the far side of the room, peering deep into the shadows. Owen stabbed his torch beam into the darkest areas, trying to chase out whatever had to be hiding in here. So far there were only rats – big, greasy-looking specimens swimming through the thick soup of algae, climbing out onto the tiles and running away from the torch beams.

'Come on out!' Jack called, his voice echoing. 'We've got you cornered.'

No response.

Owen slid the torch beam around again, but there was nothing. The room was empty. 'Back door?'

'We'd have heard it.'

Owen swept the torch around again. 'I don't believe it.

Nothing. It's gone. How can it have just gone like that?'

Jack slowly released the hammer on his revolver, lowering it gently with his thumb.

Owen lowered his own weapon and his stomach growled loudly. Jack gave him a look.

'I can't help it,' Owen told him. 'I'm hungry. Breakfast time.'

'It's just gone midnight, Owen.'

'I'm an early riser,' Owen shrugged. 'Besides, I'm a growing lad.'

'You poor boy.' A smile twisted Jack's lips. 'Why don't you help yourself here? You guys love your fish and chips.'

He nodded at the nearest of the water tanks, where the surface was covered with dead fish, floating in a scum of green algae. A silver sheen of dissolving scales glistened across the fetid mass. In the corner, where the corpses had gathered and started to merge into one another as they decayed, a cloud of flies broke away as the torchlight hit them. Rats stirred beneath the water, avoiding the glare.

And there was something else.

Lurking just below the surface.

As the light touched it, a long, pale shape suddenly dived, disappearing into the murky depths. Ripples spread through the scum.

'Did you see that?'

Jack stepped closer to the edge and peered into the water. 'Can't see a thing. Maybe it was a fish – a survivor?'

'No way – too big.'

Something exploded from the water, sending a fountain of brackish spray high into the air, drenching Owen and smashing straight into Jack, lifting him off his feet.

Spluttering, blinking the filthy water from his eyes, Owen brought his weapon up – but he couldn't see anything clearly enough in the darkness. He tried to bring his torch to bear, but the beam was flashing wildly and all he glimpsed was a dark shape sprawled across the floor, turning over and over as Jack wrestled with it. Then he heard a sharp cry from Jack and the heavy thud of a bone-crunching impact.

The pale shape leapt away and Owen felt something cold brush past him, so fast that he could only snatch at its slippery wetness, then – nothing. The shape disappeared into the shadows while he was still reeling. He stumbled after it, aiming again, pulling the trigger instinctively rather than with any hope of hitting anything. Two bullets zinged away into the darkness, punching plaster harmlessly out of the nearest wall, but the thing had reached the exit and was suddenly whisked away, as if by the wind.

Then silence.

Owen went back and used his torch to find Jack. He was lying on his back, teeth clenched, holding his chest. Owen knelt down and trained the light on Jack's shirt. The dark blue material was soaked in blood, a glistening stain as black as tar in this light.

'I'm OK,' grunted Jack through his teeth. 'Get after it.'

Owen shook his head. 'It's gone, mate. Took off like a crocodile with a jet-pack. Moved so fast I could hardly see it.'

'It was waiting… under the water…' Jack sat up, wincing, looking at the blood on his fingertips.

'Yeah, I got that,' said Owen ruefully. He was still dripping.

'Hell, this was a new shirt – fresh out of the packet this morning. Damn!' Jack indicated the front of his shirt, which was in tatters. Owen caught a glimpse of the lacerated flesh beneath.

He helped Jack to his feet. Jack limped over to the pool and looked down at the water, still swirling with dead fish and decaying matter.

'Think there's any more of them down there?' asked Owen cautiously. He hung back, making sure his gun was still cocked.

'I doubt it,' Jack said. 'We'd both be dead by now if there were. Well, you would be.'

Owen looked at him. 'You're an inspirational leader, Jack. Have I ever told you that?'

Jack grinned as he turned to leave. 'It's a gift.'

Owen stuffed his gun into the waistband at the back of his jeans and followed him. 'So we've got a Weevil-killer on the loose,' he said as they headed back to the SUV.

'Not just a Weevil-killer,' Jack replied. 'Tosh says the Rift's fluctuating because of something she calls chronon discharge – she gave me a 45-minute lecture on the subject, but basically it boils down to this: the Rift is throwing off little sparks of time energy, and, while we don't know what they mean, Tosh's computer can trace the direction these sparks travel in. One of them kept coming back here.'

'To the fish farm?'

'Two nights ago, the security guard on night duty was found dead; his body had been ripped right open from his crotch to his neck. It was quite a mess with the rats and all, but the pathologist was certain there was no way the poor guy could've been killed by another human being.'

'So they assumed it was a Weevil and called us in.'

'Got to admit, I assumed it was a Weevil too. We knew Big

Guy was active in the area after all.'

'Except that Weevils don't gut people like that. They go for the throat.'

'Actually the police pathologist reckoned on a velociraptor,' Jack grinned. 'He had some imagination, I'll give him that.'

'Dinosaurs coming through the Rift?'

'Wouldn't be the first time.'

'So what do we reckon it is, then?'

'Something that can kill a Weevil as easily as a human being.' Jack paused. 'Ianto?' His ear comm connected directly to the Hub. 'Give me some news, and make it good.'

Ianto Jones's soft Welsh voice came through loud and clear: 'Gwen and Toshiko have made it through alive.'

'Alive?'

'It was a close thing, apparently. They nearly died of boredom.'

'Right. Kinda funny, Ianto, if I wasn't in such a foul mood.'

'I take it the Weevil got away. Again.'

'Yes and no. It's a long story full of mystery, intrigue and lots of sex and violence, but the upshot is this – the Beast of Butetown is no more. Owen's bringing Big Guy in for an autopsy.'

'Ah,' replied Ianto. 'I'll be getting the Morgue ready, then.'

'Great. Any sign of Rift activity?'

'Just the "spark" trail leading to your current position. Tosh has been running an automated network program to identify any areas of temporal activity including time shifts, time warps, time jumps, time bubbles, time splits, time loops and time travel, but there's nothing unusual showing whatsoever at Evans Fish Emporium. Except, as I said, for the "spark".'

'And a Weevil ripped open like a tin of tuna,' Owen added.

'OK.' Jack clicked his tongue, considering. He kept looking around the old warehouse. Eventually he sighed and said, 'Ianto, you can liaise with the cops. Sergeant Thomas is the guy in charge here. Tell him I want this entire area cordoned off – armed guards until further notice. Then get the coffee on. We're coming back to base.'

Jack yanked open the door of the SUV. He looked over the top of the car at Owen. 'Initial assessment?'

'I'll know more when I've had a chance to look at Big Guy properly.'

Jack started the SUV up and reversed it across the warehouse, close to the tanks. Together they dragged Big Guy into the back of the car and closed the hatch.

When they finally climbed back into the front seats, both men were breathing hard and bone weary. Owen was soaking wet, and he could still smell the stagnant water. Mixed with the ripe odour of dead Weevil, it was enough to make him nauseous.

Jack drove out into the night and the start of a heavy downpour. The windscreen wipers started to dig holes in the rain automatically.

'At least we know what it isn't,' Owen said after a while. 'It isn't a Weevil – or a velociraptor.'

'Great, that narrows it right down: there's only a hundred billion other kinds of alien it could be. Tell you what, make out a list when we get back to the Hub and we'll work it out by a process of elimination.'

Owen sulked, too cold, hungry and tired to think of a good enough retort. Worse still, his head felt muzzy and there was a sneeze brewing. He let it out with an explosive yell, earning him another disgusted look from Jack.

'Great,' Owen muttered. 'Now I've caught a cold.'

'Well, hey, at least you caught something.'

TWO

Gwen Cooper put the back of her hand across her mouth in an attempt to hide the oncoming yawn. It was a hopeless task: the yawn was too big and too wide. Nothing could have disguised it.

'Got you,' said Toshiko Sato with satisfaction. 'You lose.'

'Sod it.' Gwen rubbed her face with her hands and then threw her thick black hair back from her face in an effort to sharpen up. 'It's not fair, anyway. You never yawn. I've never seen you yawn, not once, ever.'

They were sitting at a table in a motorway service station. It was almost deserted, but they had agreed to pull in and grab some caffeine before one or both of them nodded off in the car. They'd sat down with two large Americanos, and the yawning competition had started.

'What are we doing here, anyway?' Gwen asked, blowing into the foam on her coffee.

'Well,' said Toshiko with some enthusiasm, 'the way I like to see it, we're investigating specific chronon discharge in the area. The Rift's been fluctuating so much recently, and this seems to be a focal point for some of the more obvious temporal spasms. Jack's doing the same thing near the city centre.'

Gwen blinked at her. 'I was speaking philosophically.'

'Ah.' Toshiko had already taken out one of her scanning instruments, ready to demonstrate. She smiled quickly and returned it to her bag. 'Philosophy. Not my strong point. Quantum physics and Stephen Hawking, yes. Metaphysics and Plato, not so much.'

Gwen rested her chin in one hand. 'Rhys once told me that, from the moment we're born, we're all on a collision course with death.'

'If that's philosophy then I'll stick with Hawking.'

'I think he read it somewhere in a novel. That's why he's in haulage, not philosophy. But it's true, though, when you think about it. We're all going to die some day.'

'Well, all of us except Captain Jack Harkness, it seems.'

Gwen nodded slowly. 'The exception that proves the rule.'

Toshiko thought about it for a while. 'I suppose it does mean that one day, for the rest of us, we really will breathe our last breath. Say our last word. Think our last thought…'

'The final act.'

'You sort of stop thinking about it in our line of work,' Toshiko said. 'We've each faced "the final act" so many times, it just becomes—'

'Part of the routine?'

'—an occupational hazard.'

'I had that already in the police,' Gwen mused. 'Rhys used to worry about it a lot. God knows what he would think if he knew what I did now.' She stared into space for a long moment. 'Poor Rhys…'

'This is getting too maudlin,' Toshiko warned. 'A motorway services at midnight is no place to think these thoughts. You and Rhys are fine, you're strong, you're getting married. It's good that you have a life outside Torchwood. None of the rest of us have that, not really.'

'I suppose.' Gwen sat up straight, brushed her thick black hair away from her face. 'OK, non-philosophical question: what are we doing here, exactly? Something about chronic somethings, wasn't it?'

Toshiko smiled patiently. 'Chronons are discrete particles of time. The Rift has been throwing them out like little sparks for some time. I don't know if it's anything to do with the recent time shift with 1918 but…' Her smiled faded, just a little, as she remembered what it had taken to put things right then. The final act, once again. She looked down at her coffee and said nothing.

'Hey,' Gwen reached out, squeezed her hand. 'Chronon particles. Tell me more.'

Toshiko blinked, shook her head and considered the subject. 'It's not easy to explain. I've been monitoring the fluctuations in the Rift. I don't know if it's some sort of natural adjustment, like an aftershock or a hiccup, or whether something else is directly affecting it. But the results are plain to see: tiny threads of temporal activity all over the region, spreading out much further than usual.' She sipped her coffee, licked the tiny line of froth from her lip. 'Which is why we've ended up here, I suppose…'

'Chasing ghosts,' Gwen smiled. 'Strange sightings in the mists near Newport… Spookiness in Splott…' She opened her eyes wide. 'Who ya gonna call?'

'Torchwood!'

They laughed and then quickly stopped, embarrassed at their loudness. It was gone midnight and there were only three other customers here. One of those looked like a vagrant; baggy black cords, trainers, old parka with the hood up. As Gwen looked the old guy over, he suddenly turned his head towards her and she visibly flinched. He had dark eyes but she could see them clearly in the shadows of his hood, almost burning like coals.

'What's up?' asked Toshiko.

Gwen shrugged. 'I dunno; just getting jumpy I suppose. I was checking out that old guy and he caught me eyeballing him.'

Toshiko sneaked a look, took in the scruffy coat, scratchy grey beard and dark, dangerous eyes. The fingers which poked out of the sleeves of the parka were grubby, and there were big smudgy thumbprints on his tea mug, visible even from here. As Toshiko watched, the man dredged up some phlegm from the back of his throat and spat it out into the cup.

Toshiko turned back to Gwen and leaned in, talking quietly. 'Well,' she said slowly and carefully, 'maybe he fancies you.'

Gwen barked out a loud, unladylike laugh, and the four other people in the cafe all looked up. 'Tosh, that is just – eww, no!' Gwen screwed up her face and tried not to laugh again.

'Don't look now,' smiled Toshiko, 'but he's still watching you…'

'No, you're wrong,' Gwen argued, grinning. 'He's watching you. Hey, I think you're in there, Tosh!'

The man was going through another series of coughs. Too many fags. Gwen drained her coffee, stood up and collected her bag, slinging it over a shoulder. 'C'mon, let's go.'

Toshiko nodded in the old man's direction. 'What about…?'

'You can have him if you like. He's not my type.'

'Too dirty?'

'Not dirty enough.'

Laughing raucously again, the two women headed for the exit. Toshiko held out her hand and asked Gwen for the car keys. 'You're too tired to drive. I'll take us back.'

'Won't argue with that.' Gwen paused to fish in her bag for the keys and, as she did so, drew level with the old man's table. He reached up and put a hand on her arm and she jumped again.

'Whoa,' he said, showing the palms of his hands. 'No offence, girl. I just wanted to tell you…' He nodded back in the direction they'd come. 'You left your purse on the table.'

Gwen looked back and swore. Nestled between the coffee cups, the remains of a doughnut and a few screwed-up napkins was the red leather of her wallet. 'Thanks,' she said, and hurried back to fetch it.

'You want to be careful with things like that,' the old guy warned Toshiko. 'Crooks these days want more than just cash. They want credit cards and everything. They steal identities too, y'know.'

'Yes,' said Toshiko. 'I know.'

'Like *Invasion of the Bodysnatchers*,' the old man continued. He coughed again and rubbed at his chest. 'You ever see that film? Pod people. That's what they called 'em. Now they're just crooks like all the others.'

'Thanks again,' said Gwen as she returned. The old guy nodded and scratched his beard with a grubby forefinger. Gwen wondered if she should give him something, but

Toshiko gave a minute shake of her head and urged her towards the door.

'Just before you go…' said the old guy, raising his voice slightly.

Gwen stopped. 'Here we go, he wants money,' she thought, reaching for her purse.

But he shook his bushy head and held up a hand. 'Keep your cash, love. Not interested. Money don't mean nothing to me. I didn't get where I am today by having money.'

'Well, no,' agreed Gwen.

He cleared his throat. 'If Torchwood really is looking for ghosts, you should try Greendown Moss. It's haunted.'

Toshiko gaped. 'Did you just say Torchwood?'

He stood up, towering over both women. 'Don't look so startled. I know all about Torchwood.' He suddenly roared with laughter. 'The look on your faces! He said it'd be priceless, and he was right. He was always right!'

'I beg your pardon?' said Gwen.

The man gave another laugh, full of warmth. 'How is Cap'n Jack these days? Still looking like he's dodging forty? Still going misty-eyed whenever someone mentions the war? I bet he's still addicted to Glenn Miller and wearing that old greatcoat!'

Gwen smiled despite herself. 'You know Jack.'

'I only ever knew him as Captain Jack. A damned fine man, even if he did wear boots with turn-ups. American, too, but that's not his fault, is it? He was a glory-hunting maniac and the kindest man I ever knew. Saved my life twice in '73, and then left me for a chorus girl from Boston. Give the smooth-talking bastard two fingers from me next time you see him.'

'Uh, right,' Gwen nodded.

'Anyway,' the man carried on regardless, 'I owe him a favour or two, don't I? And he sent a message to say you two would be coming this way. A looker and a genius, he said. Which one's which?'

Toshiko and Gwen exchanged another glance.

'I'm an unnatural historian,' continued the old man, not waiting for a reply. 'Been studying the area and its ghosts and ghoulies for the last fifty years. Professor Leonard Morgan, at your service. You can call me Professor Len.'

THREE

Gwen pulled the Saab over to the side of the road and switched off the engine.

'Now ain't that a beautiful sight,' said Professor Len softly. He was leaning forward, between the front seats, looking out at the sunrise. The sky was a brilliant eggshell blue, streaked with a dozen wide strips of orange and lilac cloud. The sun was low, little more than a glare on the horizon, and beneath it was a vast sea of mist. A distant line of bare winter trees cast long, ghostly shadows.

The professor scratched his beard and let out a low, appreciative whistle, causing both Gwen and Toshiko to wrinkle their noses. It was far too early for beer breath. 'One touch of nature makes the whole world kin.' He looked at Toshiko and winked. 'That's Shakespeare, that is. Just showing off my education, see. Just so you know you're not the only genius in the car.'

'So you've decided I'm not the looker?' Toshiko observed acidly.

'Don't worry, girl, I go for brains over beauty every time.'
He looked apologetically at Gwen. 'No offence, mind.'

Gwen was grinning at Toshiko. 'None taken.'

'You're sure this is the place?' Toshiko asked, leaning
slightly away from the professor with a sour expression.

'Of course I am. I was brought up around here.'

Gwen was checking the OS map. They were miles from
any main roads. 'Yep, here it is: Greendown Moss. Marshland,
mainly. We should have brought our wellies.'

They got out, the two women wrapping their coats around
them to keep out the cold. Professor Len stood and watched as
Gwen locked the car. Away to the right was a long, undulated
field covered with a blanket of grey mist and ringed by silver
birch rendered almost invisible in this weather.

'Is it safe to walk across?' Toshiko asked.

Professor Len shrugged. 'If you know what you're doing.
It can be treacherous, though. You've got to treat it with
respect. Greendown Moss is what's known as a floating bog:
it's basically a great raft of peat floating on a lake. It's over
fifty feet deep. It's dangerous because, although you can walk
on most of the peat quite easily, there are holes in it that you
can't see – thin patches where a person can just slip right
through.'

'Sounds lovely,' said Gwen.

'But what about the ghosts?' asked Toshiko. 'Where do
they come into it?'

'Ah,' said Professor Len. 'Local legends. A woman – a witch
– is said to haunt this place. They call her Sally Blackteeth. She
lurks in the ditches and drags the unsuspecting traveller down
into the bog. Men, mostly, it has to be said. Pulls them all the
way down to the bottom and drowns them – if they're lucky.

You can sometimes see her around these parts, wandering the Moss, looking for her next victim.'

Gwen and Toshiko watched the thin mist rolling across the bog. In was unnaturally quiet out here – there was no traffic and all they could hear was the occasional, distant cry of the ravens in the spectral trees. Otherwise it was silent.

'Let every bird sing its own note,' whispered Professor Len, his eyes closed, listening as though he was at an opera.

'What do you mean, "if they're lucky"?' asked Gwen loudly and clearly.

The eyes snapped back open. 'Sometimes Old Sally would take a man down into the bog to live with her and have her babies. Fate worse than death, that. Dunno how she did it, mind, but I guess she can do it if she's a witch.'

Gwen and Toshiko were both smiling at him now, amused by his earnestness. He coughed and scratched his beard fiercely. 'Some of her victims she throws back, when she's finished with 'em, as a warning to others – to stay away.' He looked sideways at them and then shrugged. 'It's up to you if you want to believe it or not. But you're Torchwood, so anything goes.'

'We like to keep an open mind,' nodded Gwen.

'I've seen Sally,' the professor said. 'She often comes here. Water hags tend to keep to their own patch. Black Annie, who lived in the Dane Hills of Leicestershire, used to live in a cave. She dug it out herself with claws as hard as iron and decorated it with the skins of the children she ate.'

'That's nice.'

'They can be vicious, but they can also be fair. They're sometimes called grindylows in Yorkshire. There was one there who took a man to be her husband, lived in a ditch with him for two years before his wife came and asked for him back. The grindylow agreed, but said she could only have him back if she could swap him for someone else. So the wife tricked another man into the ditch and got her husband back. The grindylow changed her mind because she didn't like the replacement, so she let him go. He went and found the wife and her husband and murdered them both in their bed out of revenge. Seemed a bit mean-spirited, that, I always thought.'

'You're full of charming stories, aren't you?'

'Oh, I know all of them. And what's more they're all perfectly true.'

'And you say you've met this Sally Blackteeth person?'

'Seen her. You've got to be careful, though. She doesn't always look the same way twice. She's got a bit of the bogie in her.'

'Bogie?'

'Shape-shifting spirits which torment menfolk. More common than you think.'

'When does the Sally Blackteeth story date from?' Toshiko asked. 'Middle Ages?'

'Oh, yeah, from right back then. But they reckon the last man to be dragged down to his death by Sally was in 1974.'

'Really?'

'They never did find his body. It's probably still down there, rotting away.' Professor Len smiled and gave Gwen a nudge with his elbow. 'Food for the worms – and company for Sally, probably.'

Toshiko had taken a small, hand-held device out of her coat pocket and scanned the field. It could easily have been mistaken for a sophisticated mobile phone, because that is what it had once been. Toshiko had redesigned it to accommodate a smart piece of alien kit that helped to track warps in the Earth's localised time field, and she used it now to scan for alien technology or recent movements through the Rift.

Professor Len eyes the device suspiciously. 'What's that, then? Ghost detector?'

'Sort of.' The little machine flickered with coloured lights like a miniature Christmas decoration. It bleeped and whirred as Toshiko studied the readings on the tiny screen. 'Yep – got something,' she announced as the device squawked. 'Directly ahead; no, a little to the north east, about two hundred yards.'

'Come on, then,' said Gwen, starting forward.

'Wait a minute,' said the professor. 'You can't go across there. You don't know the safe routes.'

'Then you lead the way.'

'Are you completely mad? I'm not giving Sally Blackteeth any chances. I'm staying right here.'

'Don't tell me you really believe those stories!'

He stared at her. 'Of course I believe the stories. So should you. What kind of staff is Jack taking on these days?'

'Only the best,' Gwen replied. 'OK, fine. Stay here by the car. You can watch.'

The old man looked appalled. 'Don't be daft, girl. I didn't think you were coming here to walk across the Moss. I thought you were only coming to look.'

'Gwen, we have to hurry if we want to investigate properly,' Toshiko said, studying the monitor intently. 'The temporal trace could fade any moment.'

Gwen smiled at Professor Len. 'We'll say hello to Sally if we see her.'

'Never mind her,' he said. 'It's the bog you've got to look out for.'

Toshiko was already climbing down from the roadside, stretching a leg across a ditch to reach the moss. 'Gwen, come on...'

'Just take it easy,' advised Professor Len, admitting defeat. He clearly knew better than to bother arguing with the two young women. 'Keep to the firm ground, where the moss is. Don't step anywhere you don't like the look of.'

Gwen hopped down after Toshiko and led the way. The ground was hard and firm for the first few metres, but then it suddenly became noticeably softer – there was a discomforting springiness underfoot, almost as if they were walking across a bed. The ground gurgled and burped beneath the thin mist swirling around their ankles.

Toshiko followed, scanning all the time. 'Keep going... directly ahead...'

'Any idea what it is?' Gwen asked.

'Definite time disturbance – that means Rift activity. Must be something odd to be this far out.'

'Tell me we're nearly there, because this mud is getting right on my nerves, not to mention my trainers. I think they're letting in water.'

'Keep going,' Toshiko said. Their feet squelched through the soft earth as they continued.

'Remember what Professor Len said; keep to the firm ground. We don't want to drop through any holes.'

'It's hardly likely. This area is heavily saturated, but it should support our weight. There may be pools, but they'll be visible. Just be careful and try to keep to the path...'

Gwen watched the ground in front of her carefully as they

crept forward. 'I can't see any path.'

'It'll be the route across the marsh used by animals. The grass will be pressed down. The reeds will be growing in the wettest parts.'

'Think I've just found one of the wettest parts.' Gwen let out a groan of dismay as her right foot disappeared up to the ankle in cold water. She aimed the torch and saw mud swilling over her shoe as she pulled it back out. 'Yuck.'

'Wait – it's just up ahead,' murmured Toshiko, holding up the scanner. 'Look, chronon discharge and a fair degree of localised plasma streaming as well…'

'You've lost me.' Gwen turned and waved to Professor Len, who was still watching from the road. He was only just visible now, a distant grey figure standing by the car. He saw her and waved back.

'More chronon discharge,' said Toshiko, and there was a note of caution in her voice now. 'Something up ahead, in the mist.'

Automatically, Gwen drew her gun. It was a semi-automatic, Torchwood-customised with laser sights. She brought the weapon up and quickly found the tiny red dot of light in the grass ahead of them, reflecting from the dips and pockmarks where water gathered in wide, shallow puddles among the reeds.

'What makes you think it's hostile?' whispered Toshiko.

'Experience.'

'You may have a point.' Toshiko raised the scanning device, made a few alterations to the controls. The scanner bleeped and she studied the readings on the little screen, her soft features lit by its blue luminescence. 'But these readings… they're not like anything we've picked up before.'

They'd reached a standstill in the middle of the field. Gwen stood with her back to Toshiko, gun arm outstretched. Toshiko fiddled with the scanner, muttering technical responses to herself as she worked.

'So what d'you reckon it is, then?' Gwen whispered. It was so quiet here – silent, in fact, except for the two of them and the softly gurgling earth.

'I don't know. But it's out there and moving.'

Gwen gripped the automatic tighter, tried to keep her breathing slow and regular. No point in panicking. Yet.

'Ten o'clock,' Toshiko said quietly.

Gwen switched her aim, momentarily losing track of the laser dot.

'Eleven.'

Gwen twitched the gun to her right. Still nothing. She looked back towards the road, but there was no sign of Professor Len in the mist now.

'Want to go back to the car?' said Toshiko.

'No way. I want to know what the hell this is.'

'So Torchwood. No wonder Jack loves you.'

'What?'

'No wonder Jack loves having you on the team. He saw it straight away – saw that you were a natural, like the rest of us.'

'Yeah, well, that doesn't mean I'm not scared.'

'Twelve o'clock. It's circling us.'

Gwen started forward, trudging through the mud, ignoring the cold water splashing around her ankles. She'd had enough of standing still and being scared; it was time to move in and do something.

Gwen had gone no more than ten paces before Toshiko

44

called out after her. 'It's gone.'

'What?' Gwen turned, swinging the torch beam around, finding Tosh. 'What d'you mean, gone?'

Toshiko held up the scanner. 'It's blanked. Whatever was here has just disappeared.'

Gwen frowned and then turned slowly back, keeping the gun up, staring into the darkness. 'No it hasn't.'

'Scanner's not registering, Gwen...'

'Doesn't mean it's gone. Doesn't mean it's not here.' Gwen lowered her voice to a whisper. 'It's just hiding.'

Toshiko caught up with her with a series of little splashes. 'The scanner doesn't work like that...'

'You said yourself it's not like anything we've seen before. Maybe it can block the scanner, or scramble the readings or something.'

Silence.

'Tosh?'

'Gwen, I'm sinking.'

She turned and found Toshiko looking almost comically short besides her. She shone the torch down at her feet and found the mud rising up to Toshiko's knees. Instinctively Gwen stuffed her gun into a back pocket and then grabbed hold of Toshiko.

'I thought you said there wasn't any quicksand,' said Gwen. She wasn't panicking yet, but she needed to get Toshiko out of the mud.

'It's marsh,' Toshiko said. 'Remember, some patches are firm, other patches grow over deep water. I must have stepped off the path.'

'Can you try to step out?'

'What do you think I'm doing?' There was a hint of real

anxiety in Toshiko's voice now. 'I can't move my feet. I'm sinking!'

Gwen looked back at the road. She couldn't even see the car any more let alone the professor; but then she heard him – heavy splashes through the mud and a tall, lurching figure emerging like a caveman from the mist. He had seen Toshiko in trouble and was coming to help.

'Keep still!' she heard him call.

Gwen turned back to Toshiko. 'Keep still,' she urged. 'Professor Len's coming now.'

There was a horrible silence for a few moments as Toshiko sank slowly into the water. Gradually they heard the professor's footsteps splashing towards them. He caught up, winded, panting, and immediately grabbed Toshiko around the waist. 'Come on, girl! Up you come!'

But no matter how hard Gwen and Professor Len pulled, the mud just continued to suck Toshiko down. The rate of descent was becoming inexorable and she was starting to panic. 'Gwen, it's really cold! I'm sinking! Help me!'

'We're doing our best, girl!' grunted Professor Len. His face was red with the effort above his beard.

Gwen moved around so that she could put her arms under Toshiko's shoulders and heave. She strained hard but there was no moving her.

'Lie down,' gasped the professor, shifting position as well. He couldn't get any decent leverage because he was trying to make sure he didn't step on the same patch of marsh that Toshiko had. If they both got stuck there was no way out.

'What?'

'Lie down, spread your surface area across the moss,' the professor instructed. 'You won't sink so fast.'

Toshiko looked at him wide-eyed. 'Lie down? Are you mad?'

'It's OK,' Gwen assured her, but she felt far from confident. Her own heart was thudding madly in her chest. 'Lie down, quickly!'

Awkwardly, Toshiko started to lower herself towards the ground, into an uncomfortable squatting position.

'You need to lie down flat, like you're floating on the surface of a swimming pool,' the professor urged.

Gingerly, Toshiko lowered herself even further, her face a mask of fear and revulsion. She was already soaked to the skin, a thick brown tidemark rising up the white top she was wearing beneath her leather jacket. Carefully Gwen moved around until she was behind her, checking each step, probing with the flat of her foot to see if the mossy ground would take her weight. 'Lean back to me, and I'll see if I can pull you out,' she said. 'It may be easier at this angle.'

Once again Gwen got a good grip under Toshiko's arms and heaved. At first she seemed immovable, but then, with a sudden wet sucking noise, Toshiko slid out of the marsh's grip and both Gwen and Professor Len fell backwards, dragging her with them.

They lay on the wet ground for a minute, Gwen gasping and laughing with relief. Professor Len was less amused. 'I told you not go out on the moss!' he roared. 'You could've been killed!'

Toshiko crawled weakly away from the mud, shivering in the cold.

And then stopped.

'Gwen.'

Gwen twisted around. 'What is it?'

Professor Len had already seen it. He climbed slowly to his knees, his eyes wide in shock and horror.

'Look.' Toshiko's face was drawn and mud-stained, but there was a look in her dark eyes that had an immediate, sobering effect on Gwen.

There was a face in the mud. Emaciated skin was stretched tight over the skull, yellow teeth bared as if with the strain of coming to the surface. The crusty eye sockets were full of silt and worms.

'It was right beneath me,' Toshiko whispered, her voice trembling. 'Under the water all this time.'

'We must have disturbed it,' Gwen said, bending over for a closer look. 'It's male. Look – there's the rest of the body, half-submerged. He was probably trapped under the moss. The struggle freed the corpse and it floated to the surface.'

Suddenly Toshiko was fumbling for her scanner. Her muddy fingers slid all over the controls but in a few more seconds she had it working again. 'Chronon discharge,' she said. 'Signs of Rift fluctuation.'

'No,' said Professor Len, shaking his head fearfully. 'It's Sally Blackteeth. She's coughed him back up from the depths.' He looked up at them, his eyes wide and staring, full of fear. 'It's a warning!'

FOUR

Bob Strong went to see Iuean Davies first thing in the morning. The practice manager was sitting in his office with his feet up on the desk, aiming balls of screwed-up paper at the waste basket.

'What's up?' he asked as Bob opened the door without knocking and strode in. 'Can't find your manners?'

'Sorry. Problem.'

'You look bloody terrible. Lay off the booze.'

'No, it's not that. I had a rough night – didn't get much sleep.'

'Don't tell me: you've fallen madly in love with Letty Bird, and you can't bear to tell her yourself. You've lain awake all night thinking about her. You're bursting with this mad, dark and dangerous passion and you want me to tell her for you. Am I right?'

Bob closed the door carefully behind him and leant against it, arms folded. 'I had Saskia Harden in my surgery yesterday morning.'

Iuean swung his feet off the table, eyes wide. 'My God, free tickets to see Wales v England and then you get to have Saskia Harden in your bloody surgery too. You really do get all the luck.'

'I mean she came to see me.' Bob wasn't in the mood for schoolboy jokes, although he did manage a faint smile after a moment's consideration. 'Actually, I could have had her. But I didn't.'

'Ah, professional detachment,' Iuean murmured. 'Only to be admired – but never practised. At least, that's my motto. So – what did the Angel of Death want this time? Hurled herself off any tall buildings recently? Thrown herself under a bus?'

Bob shrugged. 'I think her suicidal days are behind her – if they were ever there in the first place. I still have my doubts.'

Iuean scoffed. 'Oh, come on! The police fished her out of Rhydwaedlyd Brook. Face down. She's lucky to be alive. The paramedic actually pronounced her dead, if you remember the report. Frightened the life out of everyone when she sat up cool as a cucumber in A&E.'

'She frightens the life out of me, to be honest.'

'Rubbish. She's a bit odd, that's all.' Iuean reconsidered for a moment. 'OK, she's got issues, shall we say. But, in the end, she's just a woman, and they all have issues. She's good looking. Available. What are you waiting for?'

'I don't actually know. But something's not right. She says she's never tried to commit suicide, not even once.'

'The evidence would indicate otherwise.'

'I'm not convinced. There's more to her than meets the eye.'

Iuean let out one of his big laughs. 'Bob Strong, the eternal romantic! You know what your trouble is, don't you? Besides being English?'

'Yes.'

'There's a medical term for it, actually. It's called Hugh Grantism. You spend so long faffing around trying to do the correct thing that the chance to do anything at all just slips you by.'

'I think she needs help,' Bob said. 'It's just I'm not sure what with.'

'You are now officially wasting the practice manager's time. You are the weakest link, goodbye.'

Bob coughed, fishing for his handkerchief. 'Oh no,' he said miserably. 'That's all I need. Reckon I've caught a cold. Felt it coming on yesterday.'

'Well no bloody wonder!' Iuean leant back from his desk, balancing his chair on two legs and putting his hands behind his head. 'Something's definitely going around. I've had six chest infections and four cases of flu since Monday. And that's not including all the usual bloody sore throats and sniffles.'

Bob could feel that tickle building in his own throat and quickly cleared it. The cough stung.

'So what's the matter?' Iuean asked. 'Come on, I need to write up some notes and make a cost breakdown for the new practice nurse. I haven't got all day to waste on you coughing your guts up in my office and mooning over that bloody woman.'

'I'm not mooning over her!'

'You fancy her, don't you?'

'Well I'm not sure. I think I do, yes.' Bob looked up apologetically. 'Is that right? Should I? She's a patient, after all.'

'Hardly. So she's registered with you and she's been to see you a few times. So what? She's single, isn't she? No bloody relatives or next of kin as far as I remember from her notes. Bloody well up for it as well, from what you've told me. Go for it!' Iuean sat forward, suddenly serious. 'Maybe a personal relationship, rather than a professional one, is just what she needs. Have you thought of that? I can tell by your vacant expression that you have not. Well, do think about it. Some problems can't necessarily be solved in the consulting room. Go on, see her, ask her out. Talk to her as Bob Strong, not Dr Strong. Or do you think the ex-Mrs Strong wouldn't approve?'

'It's not that. She's just a bit... well, as you said. Odd.'

'She's a woman! What do you expect? Normality?' Iuean tutted impatiently. 'You're setting your standards too bloody high, boyo, that's your trouble. Get in there while she's still interested, you fool.'

'Yeah. Maybe you're right.'

'I always am. I have two perfect marriages and two perfect divorces behind me to prove it.'

'Thanks.' Bob coughed again and searched for his hanky, only to find his trouser pockets empty. 'I'll think about it,' he said. His throat was sore now and he decided to take some aspirin himself. He gave Iuean a small salute and headed back to his own surgery.

On the way past the reception desk, he stopped and spoke to Letty Bird. 'Did Saskia Harden make an appointment for next week?'

'Not that I'm aware of.'

'I did tell her to stop at the desk on her way out and make one.'

'Well, she didn't.' Letty tapped at some keys on her computer and swivelled the screen so that Bob could see.

'There. Blank. At least, as far as Ms Harden is concerned. All you've got for this time next week – so far – is Mrs Finnigan's bunions and the check-up on Mr Grundy. The scans should be back from the hospital by then, and you can tell him the good news. Or the bad news, depending on what the results are.'

'I can hardly wait.' Bob thought for a moment and then said, 'Do we have Ms Harden's phone number on file?'

Letty raised her severely plucked eyebrows.

'I need to check something with her.' He knew just the kind of sucked-lemon look a request like this would provoke, but he was determined to follow this through now.

Tight-lipped, Letty worked the keyboard and then frowned. 'No. We don't have any contact telephone number for her. Does she even have a phone?'

Bob shrugged. 'Apparently not.'

'Doesn't have an address either by the looks of it. At least not one that makes sense. I know the Marshfield area. There's no such place as this.' She tapped the screen.

'OK.' Bob thanked her for nothing and turned towards his surgery, rubbing his chest painfully as he coughed again.

'You should see a doctor!' Letty called after him.

FIVE

Jack took out his frustration on the Hub's firing range. He aimed the Webley one-handed, putting a single round through the chests of four separate Weevils and the final two bullets through the forehead of the last.

Owen peered into the dingy shadows at the far end of the disused underground tunnel. They kept it gloomy to make it more difficult. 'That one was an inch high.'

'So what? It's dead, isn't it?'

'Oh, yeah, dead as a cardboard cut-out with two bullet holes in it can be…'

Jack lowered the revolver and clicked open the cylinder. 'So what's your problem?'

'Real targets don't stand still. And even if they do stand still, the first round will knock them back. The second round will miss.'

Jack quickly reloaded. 'Not me, buddy.'

'You're tired.'

'Like I said – not me.' Jack cast him a sideways glance. 'Get anything from Big Guy?'

'Not much. The wound was deep and lethal; you know that already. He never stood a chance. The damage to the internal organs was traumatic and consistent with a single, raking slash directed upwards from the crotch to the sternum. I imagine it must have made his eyes water somewhat.'

'So what are we talking about? Some kind of predator?'

'Unlikely. As far as we know, Weevils have no natural predators, although that is supposition on our part. We know so little about them, really. But a natural predator only ever kills to eat – and there was no sign of anything snacking on Big Guy.'

'Could it have been disturbed?'

'It's possible. But somehow I doubt it.' Owen let out a huge yawn he made no effect to conceal. 'I've put him in the Morgue anyway.'

'I thought you were going to get your head down? You look like you could do with some kip.'

Owen pursed his lips. He didn't bother arguing. He was certainly tired, but he was still too wound up after the action in the warehouse. There was no way he was going to get to sleep now, and he didn't feel like going home. Besides which, time on the firing range was always fun, and he knew perfectly well that Captain Jack Harkness could put six bullets through the same diamond on a playing card at this range. Even using that old relic of a handgun. Owen didn't know why Jack was so attached to it; the weapons Torchwood had available were literally incredible; a lot of them were state-of-the-art firearms and many were augmented with alien technology. They had automatics that couldn't miss, laser-guided rounds, explosive rounds, depleted uranium rounds, stun-guns, handguns that carried super-dense flechettes in a slim magazine containing nearly 200 shots. And yet Jack always stuck with his old Webley revolver, its grip worn smooth with years of usage and the flat-sided barrel nicked with a lifetime of action. He kept it in a large, old-fashioned leather holster at his hip.

Another six shots thundered down the range and punched flakes of paper into the damp air. Each round had struck the first three Weevil cut-outs in the eye.

Jack stood in a slowly moving cloud of gun smoke, arm extended, face stony.

'Coffee, gentlemen,' said Ianto as he came in. He put down the tray on one of the reloading tables and brushed a smudge of cordite from his shirt cuff. He looked up, saw Jack's grim expression, then checked the Weevils. 'Feeling a bit out of sorts, are we?'

'I didn't like the way they were looking at me.'

Owen smiled at Ianto and jabbed a finger at Jack. 'He's frustrated, he is.'

'I know. He always aims high when he's in a bad mood.'

'You could both do with some practice yourselves,' said Jack. 'I want you all on this firing range at least once a day from now on.'

'What's the big hurry?' Owen asked.

'I don't know – yet.'

'It's the Rift, isn't it?' said Ianto. 'All these fluctuations and sparks. Something's coming and we don't know what it is.'

'You gotta be ready,' said Jack simply. He was wearing a fresh, pale blue shirt over his white tee. There was, predictably, no sign of any wound now. 'Tell me about Gwen and Tosh. What's new?'

'They're checking out a new lead, ' replied Ianto. 'Not far

from Newport, somewhere called Greendown Moss.'

'New lead?' prompted Owen.

'Professor Len is with them,' Ianto said.

'Professor Len?' Owen looked confused. 'Sorry, have I missed something?'

'An old acquaintance,' Jack explained. 'Historian and ghost hunter. Thought he could be useful.'

'Well three cheers for Professor Len,' said Owen. He turned and whispered to Ianto, 'Never heard of him.'

'Let's hope they have more luck than we did, anyway.' Jack reloaded his gun, slipped it back in its holster and closed the flap down over the butt. He picked up his coffee, sipped it, then talked as he walked, heading for the exit. 'Course, they have a slightly trickier job: they don't know exactly what they're looking for either, but at least they don't know where to look. What's our excuse?'

Owen cleared his throat. 'Poor light. Couldn't see a thing in that bloody warehouse. I almost shot you.'

'We had it cornered, Owen.' Jack made his way through the Hub to his own office and sat down, swinging his boots up onto the desk.

'Whatever it was,' said Ianto.

'There was no way out,' Jack continued. 'The damn thing just disappeared.'

'Teleport?' wondered Owen.

'Anything's possible. But it didn't feel like that – and besides there's usually an energy residue, a tang in the air you can taste when a matter transmitter's in use.' Jack's blue eyes narrowed as he thought. 'I want it found, guys. I don't like the idea of an unidentified extraterrestrial loose in Cardiff. There are too many identified ones here already. And if anything's coming in through the Rift we don't know about, I want to know why.'

Owen stood at the hand rail, overlooking the Rift, which ran through Cardiff like an invisible dagger. It was symbolised by the huge water sculpture which stood outside the Millennium Centre and ran directly underground to the base of the Torchwood Hub. Down here the monolith had lost a lot of its shine to corrosion and algae, and parts of the complex machinery inside were open to view, but it was still impressive.

If the Rift was a blade, then the wound it had made bled problems – flotsam and jetsam and alien life forms from across time and space, all washed up on the South Wales coast. It was Torchwood's job to find them, track them down, neutralise any potential threat and, if possible, use what they found to arm the human race against the future. The only trouble being that the future was already here: this was the twenty-first century, when 'everything changes', as Jack liked to put it.

So it was a race against time, a hectic roller-coaster of a life that Owen loved. They all did.

Ianto appeared by the basin at the foot of the sculpture and waved up at Owen. 'I've checked for Rift activity,' he said. 'Tosh is the expert, but from what I can see we're having another blip.'

'Blip? Is that a technical expression?'

'Yes. As opposed to a spark.'

'Now you're just kidding me, right?'

'Activity surge,' Ianto explained patiently.

Owen jogged down the steps to join him on the way to

Toshiko's workstation. 'It's been getting busier for weeks now,' Owen muttered. 'There could be any number of things coming through that we don't know about.'

'Tosh said that there was evidence of range fluctuation as well,' Ianto said. 'Meaning that the area affected by the Rift is widening.'

'We need her back here to look at these readings,' Owen said, casting a look over the six heads-up monitors suspended over Toshiko's desk. They were all showing continuous read-outs of one kind or another. Ianto had been right: Toshiko was the expert. She could have told at a glance what was going on here. 'When's Tosh due back?'

'I assume that will depend on what they find at Greendown Moss.'

'That's out Newport way, isn't it?'

'That's where Tosh said the original Rift spike earthed, yes.' As they watched the monitors, bright green zigzags flickered across a number of display graphics. 'Another surge.'

'Give me a nice dead body any day,' Owen muttered. 'I can tell you everything then. Even if it's alien I can tell you something. But this…' he waved a hand at the glimmering screens. 'Just bollocks.'

'Is that a technical expression?'

Owen scowled. 'Get onto Tosh and Gwen, tell them to get their arses back here and do some proper work.'

'I have done some preliminary research myself,' Ianto said. 'Tried to pick up on some basic patterns in the Rift energy and cross-reference them to police reports on the paranormal.'

'Police reports? Do they have time to make reports on the paranormal?'

'You'd be surprised.'

'I thought they were too busy polishing their whistles and telling people the time.'

Ianto smiled. 'There are probably too many paranormal incidents to make a report on everything. They only report major strangeness, not minor strangeness. So they do keep records – the police are very good at that. I hacked into their database and ran a few sifting programmes to see if any minor strangenesses came up.'

'So what have you found, Sherlock?'

Ianto pushed a slim manila envelope across the desk. 'The Strange Case of Saskia Harden.'

SIX

Owen drove his Honda 2000S to Trynsel. The sat-nav prompted him quietly from the dashboard, and he was connected to the Hub hands-free via his ear comm.

'I was hoping for a day off,' he muttered ruefully as the first spots of rain appeared on the windscreen. The two-hour nap he'd taken on the sofa by his workstation already seemed like a distant memory – or a brief, unsatisfying taste of what real sleep was like.

'There are no days off at Torchwood,' said Jack cheerfully. 'What's going on?'

'Ianto's got me chasing some pretty young blonde—'

'He knows you so well.'

'—with a suicide habit.'

'Like I said. Hold it – suicide habit?'

'She keeps throwing herself in the canal,' Owen said.

'She sure sounds fun.'

Ianto's voice came through: 'Saskia Harden. Serial attempts to take her own life, according to the police reports.'

'And Torchwood is interested in her because…?'

'Filed under paranormal,' Ianto explained. 'She's been found face down in garden ponds, canals, even a lake, on no fewer than seven separate occasions in the last five months.'

'That's weird, but it's not paranormal.'

'Except that she was found dead on each occasion,' Owen added. 'You've got to admit, that's one step further than weird.'

'OK,' Jack's voice said, but there was still reservation. 'And I take it that the police didn't see this one-step-further-than-weirdness as an emergency.'

'That's correct,' said Ianto.

'So – why's Owen on his way to find her?' Jack's voice took on a warning tone. 'We're busy, Ianto. I've got Gwen and Tosh looking for ghosts in the middle of nowhere and a Weevil-killer on the loose. Then there's the young mother in Splott who's got a spider the size of a dinner plate in her bath and we're due another writ from the Hokrala Corporation any day now. We've got lots to do.'

'This Saskia girl could be a lead,' Owen said quietly.

'A lead?'

'Ianto cross-checked his non-emergency paranormal police reports with missing persons and, er, water.' Owen swallowed, realising how lame this was going to sound.

'I thought it might provide some kind of lead on your missing alien,' Ianto added. 'It went missing in the fish farm, after all. That's a water connection.'

'Kinda tenuous,' Jack said.

'Except that I back-tracked Tosh's Rift scan and found that the same kind of temporal spark that we registered at the fish farm also occurred at each of the locations where Saskia

Harden was found dead in the water.'

'You've got to admit it's probably more than coincidence,' Owen added. 'Anyway, I think she's worth checking out.'

Jack laughed knowingly. 'Yeah, after all, she's young, blonde, needs a shoulder to cry on…'

'It's a dirty job but someone's got to do it.'

'So where does she live, this mysterious and beautiful serial suicide?'

'We don't know,' Ianto admitted.

'What is she? A vagrant?'

'The address she gave the police doesn't exist,' Ianto replied. 'They don't actually know that – they'll have picked her up and transferred her to hospital and left it at that. But she doesn't feature on any government database – no birth certificate, education, national insurance, employment, taxation, or criminal record. Nothing at all. To all intents and purposes she doesn't exist. That alone is enough to warrant some investigation, but no one else has the time or, it would seem, the inclination. No one, that is, except yours truly.'

'OK,' Jack said, and there was a hint of interest in his voice now. 'So how you gonna find her?'

'Well, that's where I had to be extremely clever as well as amazingly handsome,' Ianto said. 'Because there was one, teeny-weeny little computer record which did feature Saskia Harden's name: the appointments list at the Trynsel Medical Centre.'

The Trynsel Medical Centre was a newly built NHS facility on the outskirts of Cardiff. It was a single-storey, yellow-brick building with sliding glass doors and a receptionist who only looked up at Owen after he had stood in front of the reception desk for a full forty-five seconds. He'd counted them. In that time, Owen had checked out the open-plan waiting room, with its usual array of notices advertising flu jabs, health clinics, post-natal care and sponsored fun runs. There was a large poster devoted to stopping people smoking, and another one about mental health care. Beyond these cheery signs was the waiting room proper, seemingly full of people with bad coughs. There were mothers and children, old men, one or two younger guys, but all of them were coughing and they all had grey faces and dark circles under their eyes. One old guy was making a big show of bringing up something thick and gooey from the back of his throat into his handkerchief.

'Can I help you?' asked the receptionist eventually, raising her voice over the noise.

'Yeah,' said Owen, turning casually back to look at her. 'I'd like to see Dr Strong, please.'

'You mean you'd like to make an appointment,' she stated primly.

'No, I just want to see him. It's not a medical matter.' Owen gave her a brief, tight smile. 'Well, it is a sort of medical matter I suppose. We were at uni together. He's an old mate, and I thought I'd look him up.'

The receptionist's face hardened minutely into a well-rehearsed mask of indifference. 'I'm afraid Dr Strong isn't available today.'

A large man had appeared behind the receptionist, middle-aged with a twinkle in his eye. He glanced up from the file he was reading at the mention of Strong's name.

'Someone looking for Bob?'

'Yeah – me,' said Owen quickly, before the receptionist could respond. He grinned and extended his hand towards the other man, introducing himself. 'Dr Owen Harper. Hi. I was told Bob would be here.'

'Well he would be, normally,' replied the other man. He had an ID card hanging from his shirt pocket which read Dr Iuean Davis – Practice Manager. 'In fact he was in this morning, but he's had to go home ill.'

'Typical,' said Owen. 'Something serious, I hope…?'

Davis smiled. 'Flu, I reckon. Only started this morning – nasty cough. Like most of this lot, actually.' He nodded at the waiting room full of people hacking and spluttering into hankies.

'Yeah,' mused Owen, curious despite himself. 'What's up with them?'

'Search me. It's either flu or biological warfare, I can't decide which,' Davis chuckled. 'Or maybe it's just something in the water. Anyway, I doubt Bob'll be back soon.'

'OK,' said Owen. 'No problem. I'll try him at home.'

He walked out, with the sound of the receptionist coughing behind him.

Owen climbed back into his car and contacted the Hub. 'Ianto, I need Strong's home address.'

'Problem?'

'He's not at the surgery today – he's off sick.'

'I always wondered why GPs don't take more sick leave. After all, they spend every day meeting sick people. They must catch everything going at some point.'

'Well there are plenty of them here. I've never seen such a pasty-faced bunch. What's wrong with this area? TB epidemic?'

'I'll check if you like.'

'Just give me his address. It can't be far.'

Ianto tapped up Strong's address and read it out to Owen.

'I'm on my way now. This had better be worth it.' Owen started the Honda and pulled out of the medical centre car park, nearly hitting another woman on her way in, busy coughing into a tissue.

Owen leant out the window. 'You want to look where you're going, love!'

'Sorry,' she wheezed, holding up a hand to show that she knew it had been her fault. She coughed again, a real hack, and looked down into her tissue. 'It's not the cough that carries you off – it's the coffin they carry you off in,' she said with a weak smile.

Owen nodded and drove off. He'd seen the red phlegm in the tissue. Professionally it troubled him, though the woman had been on her way to see her GP, which was the right thing to do. But the matter preyed on his mind all the way to Robert Strong's house.

It was a pleasant semi-detached with a long driveway and a Ford Mondeo. Owen rang the doorbell and waited for an answer.

Eventually a man came to the door; Owen could hear him coughing on the other side. The door opened and a long, pale face looked out. 'Yes?'

'Dr Strong?'

'Yeah. Who wants to know?'

'My name's Owen Harper.'

Strong was suddenly overtaken by a massive coughing fit, clutching the door to support himself as he doubled up.

'Here, that doesn't sound so good, mate,' Owen said,

automatically moving to help.

'It's been getting worse all morning,' Strong told him between coughs. He sounded full of phlegm. After a few moments, he recovered and smiled wanly. 'I had to come home from work today – never done that before in my life!'

'I'm a doctor,' Owen said. 'Maybe I can help.'

Strong gave a short laugh. 'I'm a doctor too,' he said. 'Fat lot of good it's done me. Come in.'

It was a bachelor's house, with black leather armchairs and a widescreen plasma TV, surrounded by untidy stacks of DVDs on the laminate flooring and a good-looking sound system. In the corner was a Wii console with a few games scattered around it. There was evidence of a previous life, however: a photo on the mantelpiece – Strong and a woman embracing, faces pressed together, grinning at the camera. Strong noticed Owen looking at it and said, 'Ex-wife. Quite liked her, then.'

'Creative differences?'

'You could say that.' Strong dissolved into more coughing and motioned towards a chair. 'Take a seat,' he croaked.

Owen sat down. 'No kids?'

'Nah, thank God.' Strong slumped into the opposite chair. 'Never got round to that – creative differences, as you say. Or procreative differences. I wouldn't have minded a couple of sprogs, but she wasn't ready for them. Career came first, she said. First, last, and always.'

There was bitterness there, but only very slight. Strong was enjoying being single. Or at least he would have been, Owen thought, if he hadn't been so ill.

'I don't know what's wrong with me,' the man confessed. 'I've never had anything like this before. Coughs and colds, yes, but this… this is something else. Reckon I've got flippin' TB.'

'That's a bit unlikely, isn't it?'

'Yeah – but not impossible. It is on the increase in the UK, has been for some years now.'

'Only in inner-city areas – and then it's the slums. But you're a long way from those kinds of places here. Have you had any tests?'

'Not yet. I'm waiting to see what happens.'

Owen smiled. 'Keep taking the tablets and come back in a week?'

Another laugh, which turned into a coughing fit. 'Yeah,' he gasped after a pause. 'That's it. I've taken some codeine for the pain; I'm just sitting the cough out.'

'Pain?'

'In the throat, when I cough. Most likely it's a bad throat infection.'

Owen nodded, thinking. He wondered whether he should say he'd stopped in at the Trynsel practice or not. But the pause in the conversation had given Strong the chance to reassess his visitor.

'You didn't say what you called for.'

'It's just routine,' Owen lied. 'When a GP goes down as quickly as you have, we have to follow it up. It's automatic.'

'We?'

'NHS Direct.' Owen had said the first thing that came into his head and instantly regretted it.

Strong wasn't impressed. 'Rubbish,' he said, and a more wary look came into his eyes.

'No, it's true. When a GP contracts a serious illness we have to investigate. Government policy now.'

'Serious illness?' There was genuine worry now. 'Do you know something I don't?'

Owen hoped serious illness was just enough to steer Strong away from asking too many questions about where he'd come from. 'Well, it's probably nothing, is it? But it's procedure. Have to be sure.'

'Sure of what?'

'That it's nothing too serious.' Hold on, this is getting daft. Nothing-too-serious? Not-serious-enough? Just-about-right-serious?

Strong leant forward, hunched over as he coughed once or twice and looked Owen carefully in the eyes. 'My boss thinks it's biological warfare, you know.'

'Why?'

'You've got to admit it makes a kind of sense. It sounds mad but it's not as unlikely as all that. What if there's been a leak somewhere, from some kind of government research facility. Look what happened last year with that foot-and-mouth outbreak – all because of some burst drainpipes in the floods. Contaminated the area where some builders were working, and then they trampled it onto the farms.' Strong sat back, his chest rumbling with another cough. 'Maybe there's something in the water. Or someone's brought this into the surgery, probably by accident, and I've picked it up.' He looked pointedly at Owen. 'And that's why you're here.'

'It is?'

'You're not from NHS Direct. You're from the Government, I can tell. Got Civil Service written all over you. Could even be MI5 – am I right?'

'If I told you, I'd have to kill you.'

Strong laughed and then coughed, long and hard, turning

red in the face with the strain of it. Owen went out into the kitchen and fetched a glass of water. By the time he got back, Strong was slumped in his chair, pale and exhausted, with flecks of spit on his chin. 'God, I feel awful,' he muttered, rubbing his chest. 'So. What happens now? Am I whisked away to a top secret research lab for tests? Or just disappeared, so no one will ever know what happened to me?'

Owen looked as though he was considering for a moment before replying. 'We may have to do some tests, yes, but you won't have to go anywhere. In fact I can take a blood sample right here, right now.' He reached into his jacket pocket and took out the field kit he always carried: a slim box no bigger than a pencil case containing needles, syringes, sterilised pads, scalpels. Some of the stuff was more advanced than the most up-to-date medical equipment available anywhere in the world.

'You came prepared,' said Strong, automatically rolling up his shirtsleeve.

'I was a Boy Scout.' Owen pulled on a pair of surgical gloves, assembled a hypodermic, sterilised a patch of skin on Strong's forearm and tapped a vein until it stood out. Then he quickly and expertly extracted some blood.

'Nicely done,' Strong said, and then coughed. 'Didn't feel a thing.'

'I'll get this analysed and then we'll know what's what,' Owen said as he stowed the kit and sample. 'But as far as we're concerned, at the moment you've just got a bad case of flu – although it could be a new strain.'

'Asian flu?'

'Doubtful, but it's really too early to tell. Like I said: tests. That'll give us an idea.'

Strong sat back, clearing his throat painfully again, thinking about the implications. He looked twenty years older. 'Bloody hell, this is just awful. How long am I going to be off work?'

'Don't worry about it,' Owen assured him, sounding positive but professional. 'Remember, this is all precautionary. It's probably nothing.'

'Yeah,' said Strong, in a hollow voice that meant he had said those same words to patients a hundred times before and not meant it either.

'Get some rest,' Owen advised him. 'I'll give you a call and let you know the results as soon as. OK?'

Strong nodded, reaching for his tissues again as another coughing fit began. He waved as Owen let himself out.

Back in the car, Owen contacted Ianto again.

'It's me. I've seen Strong and he's in a bad way. Coughing up blood. I've taken a sample for analysis and I'm on my way back now. Do us a favour and get my stuff set up.'

'As you wish.' A pause. 'And what about Saskia Harden?'

Owen swore. 'Listen, never mind her for the moment. I'm more worried about Strong. I saw another patient at the medical centre with the same symptoms, and possibly a whole lot more in the waiting room. Whatever this is, it needs prioritising.'

'Once a doctor, always a doctor, eh?'

'I'll do my job, Ianto, and you do yours. That way we all get job satisfaction.'

SEVEN

Owen found Jack on the phone to the UN in Geneva.

'Torchwood,' Jack was saying. 'Yes. T-O-R-C-H-W... look, who is this? I'm calling on a priority line, dammit, I don't need to spell anything out. I was promised a full report on the Helsinki Warp. Yes, I know that was a UNIT operation. Torchwood is copied in on everything UNIT does.' He listened for a few seconds, a muscle twitching in his jaw. 'Captain Jack Harkness. Harkness. H-A-R-K... oh, can it.'

He threw the phone onto his desk in exasperation and ran his fingers through his hair. 'What is it with these guys? Give them a desk and a phone and they think they control the world.'

'Some of them do, don't they?'

'Over my dead body. And I mean that. It's bad enough dealing with the Hokrala Corp lawyers and their ex-dimension writs, without all that United Nations red tape.' Jack leant back in his chair and called out: 'Ianto! Anything from Gwen and Tosh?'

Ianto appeared quietly and calmly at the door to Jack's office, almost as if he'd been waiting there. And he had a tray of coffee things with him. 'They should be here within the hour.'

'Great.' Jack took a coffee. 'Ianto, you always know exactly what I need. It's uncanny, I tell you.'

'That's why I work for Torchwood. Uncanny is our business.'

'You'd better get your autopsy table cleaned up,' Jack told Owen. 'Gwen and Toshiko are bringing in another guest for you.'

Owen shot Ianto a questioning look.

'They found a corpse at Greendown Moss,' Ianto explained.

'Human or alien?'

'They can't be sure. Probably human. Apparently it's rather old and somewhat decayed.'

'Two autopsies in one day. Business is good.'

'It's better than good,' Jack said. 'It's a result. According to Tosh, the corpse registers for Rift energy – it's linked to whatever's been going on with that.' He nodded towards the immense silver tower at the heart of the Hub.

Owen shook his head, then paused as his gaze fell on a decades-old poster on the wall behind Jack's head. *Coughs and sneezes spread diseases*, it read. He looked back at Jack. 'I've been thinking about Bob Strong.'

'Who?'

'The GP.'

'What about him?'

'He's very ill. He seems to think he may have been exposed to some kind of biohazard.'

Jack looked at him directly. 'Do you?'

'Can't say for certain,' Owen admitted. 'I took a blood sample, partly as cover, but mostly because I think it needs checking into.'

Jack sighed. 'Owen, this is Torchwood, not the Department of Health.' Jack swung his boots down from his desk and grabbed his coffee, heading for the door.

'The GP was only half-joking about the biohazard but I can't say for sure that he's not right,' said Owen, following Jack out. 'We've seen what can happen when an experimental strain of foot-and-mouth was accidentally released from research labs in the South of England after last year's floods, and the NHS is under siege from C-Deficile. Throw the prospect of biological terrorism into the mix and a switched-on GP could get jumpy.'

'Have you done the blood test?'

'It's running. Should be finished by now.' Owen hurried across to his workstation and punched up the test results. 'Now we can see what's what.' The screen filled with streams of chemical equations and graphs. Owen frowned, and tapped some keys. Data scrolled up the screen, and his eyes darted from side to side as he took it in. 'That's wrong,' he said quietly. 'It's gotta be...'

'What's up?' Jack joined him at the workstation.

'Doesn't make sense. The test must have mis-run.'

'Why?'

Owen tapped the screen. 'There's nothing wrong with this blood. It's perfectly normal O-negative. Cell count, blood gases, they're all spot on.'

'Which means...?'

'Whatever Bob Strong's got, it isn't a disease.' He sat

forward and typed quickly, more urgently. The screen flicked and changed and began filling up with more information. 'I've hacked into the main NHS database. It's just a thought, but… Yeah, here we go. Look at this: massive spike in respiratory complaints in the last few weeks, right across the region. Way above the seasonal average.'

'So what is it? A flu epidemic? Big deal; these people still think it's news when there's another outbreak of measles. Let me know when it's Martian Flu.'

'I told Strong it was probably a new strain of flu, but I doubt it is. And so does he, in all honesty. GPs are pretty clued up on influenza, even foreign strains of the usual A, B and C viruses. The Government has a major vaccination programme in place in case there's an outbreak or a pandemic. But this doesn't fit the flu profile.'

A quiet cough signalled Ianto's presence. 'Excuse me. I've just had word from Gwen – they've arrived.'

Jack clapped his hands. 'Great. Let's see what the cat's dragged in.'

Owen gestured at his screen. 'What about this?'

'It's still as much a matter for the medical profession as for Torchwood. I hear what you're saying, and we'll tag it for a follow up.' Jack headed towards the Autopsy Room. 'Right now, you've got another dead body to look at. Maybe you can find a connection?'

Owen bit his lip, considering the information on the screen for a second longer. Then he twisted out of his seat and followed Jack.

Gwen and Toshiko were just coming into the Hub. The strobe lights were still flashing as the massive cog-wheel vault door rolled slowly back into position behind them with its customary grinding rattle. Gwen looked tired but glad to be back at base.

Toshiko, on the other hand, just looked wet. Very wet.

Jack paused at the top of the stairs and looked down at her with a grin. 'Hey, Tosh, when I said we'd see what the cat's dragged in, I didn't think it was gonna be you!'

Owen joined him and broke into a laugh.

'Owen, don't say a word.' Toshiko glared up at him. Her face was streaked with dirt, as if she'd been lying face down in a puddle. Her hair was bedraggled and her clothes were soaked through and stained with mud. A pool of dingy water spread out across the concrete where she stood.

Ianto, with only the faintest of tuts, appeared with a number of old newspapers to put down on the floor and a clean towel for Toshiko. She thanked him icily as she took the towel and shivered. Ianto then busied himself spreading the paper out on the concrete, soaking up the water and clumps of congealed mud and grass. 'There is a doormat upstairs, you know. Several, in fact.'

'What the hell happened?' Jack asked, grinning.

'Slight accident in the marshland,' Gwen said. 'We wandered off the path at Greendown Moss. Big mistake.'

'That's a relief,' Owen said with a sardonic smile. 'For a moment I thought you'd been mud-wrestling together and I'd missed it.'

'In your dreams.'

'Only when I'm bored, girls. Only when I'm bored.'

Without another word, Toshiko went to get herself cleaned up. Gwen reported to Jack in his office.

'Your friend Professor Len was… interesting. Not your type, I'd have thought.'

'Really?'

'Sort of… grungy.'

'So he's let himself go. But he was a great guy. We had a thing together in the early seventies.' Jack smiled warmly at the memory.

'Yes,' Gwen said thoughtfully, 'he sent his fondest. But we didn't find any ghosts.'

'Ianto said you found a corpse, which is a start.'

'That was later. First we searched Greendown Moss. There was definitely something there – Tosh picked up another Rift spark, but we couldn't get a fix on it, didn't see anything.'

'Sounds familiar,' muttered Owen.

'Ignore him,' Jack told Gwen. 'He's just sore because he lost an alien in a fish farm.'

Owen pointed at himself and mouthed *I'm sore…?* incredulously.

Gwen said, 'How'd you get on with Big Guy, then?'

'He's in the Morgue. Some unidentified extraterrestrial opened him up like a—'

'So far we've had a packet of crisps and a tin of tuna,' commented Jack.

'—baked potato,' Owen finished triumphantly. He looked from one to the other. 'No?'

'Almost a meal,' said Gwen. 'Which reminds me – I'm hungry. Anyone for pizza?'

'Already ordered,' announced Ianto smoothly as he handed her a mug of hot chocolate.

'Thanks, Ianto. You are a treasure, you know that?'

He smiled. 'As a matter of fact, I do.'

'Tosh stepped off the path and got stuck in the mud.' Gwen sipped the chocolate carefully. 'At least I thought it was mud, but it turned out to be a bog or something and before we knew it she was sinking.'

Owen sniggered, shaking his head. 'Oh, I'd have paid money to have seen that.'

Gwen glared at him. 'She's lucky to be alive. If it hadn't been for Professor Len, she'd be dead.'

'Wouldn't we all?' said Jack. He stood up and clapped his hands. 'So – where's the body?'

EIGHT

Len Morgan trudged across Greendown Moss, hands deep in the pockets of his parka. It was bitingly cold out here, even at this time of year, and the wind was making his nose run continuously. Every time he put a boot down in the mud, he could feel icy fingers grabbing at his feet. For most people, a walk across the Moss would be a risky undertaking in good weather. In these conditions it was positively dangerous. Many people had met their deaths out here, and it was apparently nothing to do with Sally Blackteeth. They just sank in the mud, slipped beneath the Moss and drowned.

But not Professor Len. He knew the bog too well, and he knew Sally Blackteeth.

There was a thick mist hanging around the trees of Grey Copse. He could see the branches of the silver birch stretching up towards the white sky, but that was all. The mist closed around him as he stepped into the trees, welcoming him to another, colder, more mysterious world.

'That was a bloody stupid thing to do,' he said.

A dark figure emerged from the mist close by. 'You can talk.'

Len shivered. He knew better than to look at the figure directly. It was enough that he could hear the moist sucking noise it made as it moved slowly behind him. He never heard a footstep, only the faint, wet sound of its breath.

'I couldn't help it,' he said. 'They insisted.'

'You brought them here.'

'I had to. I owed someone a favour.'

'A favour? You don't owe anybody anything – except me.'

'This one goes back a long way. Before I met you.'

'Huh. So who is this person? The one you owe a favour to that's more important than the one you owe me. Come on – who is it?'

'You don't need to know that.' Professor Len licked his lips, sensing trouble. 'I only came to apologise. I know I shouldn't have brought them here – but you shouldn't have given them that corpse.'

'Consider it a gift.'

'They took the body back with them.'

'I expected them to.'

'It's a mistake,' Professor Len insisted bravely. 'They'll examine it, check into it.'

'Good luck to them.'

'They won't let it go. They were here for a reason. These people don't do anything without a reason.'

'Good. Neither do I.'

Len bit his lip, raised a hand to rub at his beard. He was torn with indecision, and he could sense that his next words were being waited for.

'You don't understand,' he said. 'These people – they're

special. They're unique. They call themselves Torchwood.'

There was a noise like a stake being driven into moist earth. It wasn't a gasp of surprise or shock. It was a snort of derision. 'Torchwood. I don't fear them. Never have done.'

'But they won't let it lie. Something's brought them here to the Moss. It's not you – it's some kind of disturbance in time, they said…'

Another hiss of disdain. 'They have no idea what they're dealing with.'

'I just thought you ought to know.'

'Why?'

'Because… because I want to protect you.'

'Rubbish. It's because you think I'll spare your life.'

Professor Len was trembling now, and it wasn't due to the cold. He couldn't even feel his body any more. Snot ran down his lip but he didn't even think of wiping it away. 'I don't want to die! It wasn't my idea to give them the body. You did that, not me.'

'You can't protect me. I know all about Torchwood. And I know all about Jack Harkness. He's the man you think you owe your life to, isn't he? The favour! How sweet. But it doesn't matter. It's done now.'

Professor Len swallowed, his mouth dry. 'You mean I can go?'

'Look at me.'

'No.'

'Look at me.'

Professor Len glanced up, aware that someone had moved in front of him. At first he could see nothing except the mist and the ghosts of the trees around him. There was a smell like rotting cabbage and peat mixed with the faintest trace of a butcher's yard, and then he saw his companion.

'There,' she said. 'That wasn't so bad, was it?'

He shook his head miserably. 'No,' he whispered.

'Good,' she said, smiling. And then, with one swift stroke, she sliced his neck open, deep enough to expose the vertebrae at the back, just before the blood surged up and out in a huge red fountain.

NINE

The corpse was laid out on the table in the Autopsy Room underneath a ring of brilliant exam lights. It was old and in an advanced state of decay. The skin had withered into a dark, leathery carapace stretched over wasted muscle and tendon. Some of the joints were exposed, yellowed bone just visible beneath the skein of mud that still covered the entire body.

It was still wearing the remnants of trousers and a sweater, but these were little more than scraps of material stiffened by the preserving effects of the soil. Closer examination revealed small invertebrates still making a home in the damp crevices.

The head was little more than a hairless skull with eyes crusted over behind blackened lids. The lips were partly eaten away to reveal the remains of yellow teeth.

'Definitely human,' announced Owen, now wearing his white lab coat, 'judging by the orthodontic work. Five fillings and a cap.'

He stood in the well of the Autopsy Room while the

others watched from the walkway above. There was a deck of monitoring equipment at the end of the table, and a camera filming the autopsy. Owen circled the corpse, making a number of routine observations before attempting any invasive exploration.

'The body is male, adult, although it's not possible at this stage to make a guess at its age.'

'Guess anyway,' advised Jack. He stood in his shirtsleeves, arms folded. 'You never know, you may be right.'

Owen looked up at him. 'Who, me?' he said sarcastically. He straightened up and shrugged, fiddling with the badges which speckled the lapels of his white coat. 'All right: at a very rough guess, I'd say he was aged between twenty and a hundred.'

'You're uncanny, Owen. Narrow it down.'

'Your age,' Owen said, without missing a beat.

Jack smiled but said nothing.

'Is there no way of telling who he was?' Gwen asked.

'I checked the missing persons records from the late seventies to the early eighties,' Ianto said. 'There are plenty of candidates, obviously. We need more data from the body before we can start sifting.'

'What if it was a tramp?' asked Gwen. 'They wouldn't necessarily be reported as missing, would they?'

'I hate the thought of someone never being missed,' said Ianto sadly. 'It's the ultimate humiliation, surely. So unimportant in life that no one even notices when you die.'

'Theories, anyone?' prompted Jack. He looked impatient.

'Your old mate Professor Len was telling Tosh and me about a local witch who used to drag unlucky suitors down into the bog,' said Gwen. 'According to him, the last reported victim of Sally Blackteeth went missing on Greendown Moss in 1974.'

'You think this could be him?'

'It's possible.'

Jack nodded. 'Find out. Get in touch with Professor Len.' He turned to Owen. 'Can you tell how he died?'

'That's what I'm here for,' Owen said. 'Initial observations: there's no obvious sign of violence or mutilation. No broken bones that I can detect thus far. There appears to be some swelling of the neck and throat, but it's not consistent with strangling. Probably the result of drowning.'

'He was in the middle of the marsh.'

Owen smiled humourlessly. 'Wandered off the path, got stuck in the mud. No Professor Len around to help him when he got that sinking feeling. Glug, glug, glug...'

'That could have been me,' said Toshiko quietly. She had just appeared on the steps besides Jack, having showered and changed. All Torchwood personnel routinely kept a change of clothes in the Hub in case of emergencies.

'My, doesn't she scrub up well?' said Owen.

'Leave it out, Owen,' snapped Gwen. 'She's had a bad fright.'

'Not as big a fright as this guy had,' Owen gestured at the corpse. 'The thing is, and call me Mr Boring if you must, but I don't see what's so extraordinary about this corpse. He drowned in the marsh. It's a police matter.'

'No,' said Jack firmly. 'It's a Torchwood matter. Tosh?'

Toshiko held up a hand scanner. 'Residual temporal energy all over it. If he didn't actually come through the Rift, then he was touched by something that did. That makes it our business.'

'All right,' Owen said. 'Let's have a closer look, then.' He picked up a large scalpel from the instrument trolley at his side and brandished it dramatically over the corpse like a sacrificial dagger.

'God, I bet you were unbearable at med school,' said Gwen.

'He's unbearable now,' said Toshiko, but there was the beginning of a tiny smile on her lips.

'About to make the first incision,' Owen announced, suddenly professional. It was almost as if, with the banter and playing around over, he was ready to get on with the job he loved most of all.

He approached the cadaver from the right, leaning over the chest, resting the tip of the scalpel blade against the leathery skin at the bottom of the throat in preparation for the long Y-shaped cut from sternum to navel.

At which point the corpse suddenly convulsed and screamed out loud.

Owen sprang backwards with a yell of surprise, genuinely shocked, as the corpse arched its back on the autopsy table and screamed again. It was a terrible sound: dry, parched, the result of old, decayed lungs forcing air through a withered thorax. The sound of someone jumping on a pair of old, dusty bellows. The head tilted right back, the vertebrae clicking audibly as the mouth stretched open, tearing the stiff skin which covered its cheeks. A shrivelled, blackened tongue quivered between the widening jaws as another rasping cry escaped.

Toshiko had staggered backwards at the first scream, grabbing hold of Gwen instinctively. Gwen stared at the corpse, eyes wide, utterly transfixed. Jack vaulted the chain-link rail and landed next to the autopsy table as the corpse struggled to sit upright.

'Easy, fella!' Jack shouted, holding out his hands towards the body to show he meant no harm. But it was doubtful that the thing could see at all. The eyes looked like prunes sunk inside folds of dried skin. The skull was twisting from side to side as if looking around in panic but unable to see a thing. Its mouth kept moving, trying to form words with no lips or proper tongue, leaving nothing but a series of heaving gags to emerge.

'What's it trying to say?' Toshiko asked. 'It's trying to say something!'

After a few more seconds, the corpse coughed up a mouthful of thick mud and spat it across the room, spattering the white tiles which lined the walls.

Owen climbed back to his feet, still clutching the scalpel in his white fingers. He watched in shocked fascination as the corpse tried to climb off the examination table, making incoherent shouts and cries, holding out one stiff arm as if feeling for something – anything – to touch.

Jack circled it warily, careful not to get in the way of the shower of brown spittle which burst from the thing's grinning mouth every time it tried to speak.

The skeletal fingers closed around Gwen's ankle. She was standing on the walkway, level with the corpse's head and shoulders.

'Let her go,' ordered Jack, moving closer.

But the corpse was in a rage. With an angry cry, it wrenched Gwen off her feet and she tumbled into the autopsy well, scraping her back on the edge of the steps.

Owen stepped forward and rammed the scalpel into the

corpse's neck, just where the jugular vein should be. The blade struck with a dull thud but had no discernible effect. The cadaver grabbed Gwen by the throat and pulled her upright, bringing her close enough for her to feel the gusts of fetid air blowing out of the remains of its nose and mouth.

It held her for a moment, leaning in, almost as if it was intending to kiss her. But then it became obvious that it was simply trying to look at her, to see her more closely. But its desiccated eyes were useless.

'I said let her go,' repeated Jack loudly, and this time he had his service revolver out and aimed at the corpse's head.

'Jack, it's already dead!' Owen warned.

'Maybe it needs reminding.' Jack pulled the trigger, the gun roared and a large hole appeared in the corpse's skull, exploding fragments of bone across the far wall. The corpse staggered, and, reacting instinctively, Gwen used the moment to give it a huge shove with both hands, propelling it backwards until it crashed into Owen's instrument trolley. The corpse spun around, sending the trolley flying and scattering instruments across the floor of the room.

'Told you it wouldn't work,' said Owen as the corpse continued to struggle. It had regained its feet, turning to face Jack as he walked purposefully towards it, gun arm extended.

'Wanna bet?' Jack fired again, blowing the top off the skull at point-blank range. The corpse jerked backwards, lumps of rotted brain matter dangling from the gaping hole in its cranium.

The sounds of the shots had reverberated around the hard surfaces of the Autopsy Room, leaving everyone's ears ringing. Gwen was yelling at the top of her voice, hands to her face, trying to wipe away the stinking mess from the impact of the first shot. Owen and Jack advanced on the shuddering corpse. Owen looked shocked and ashen-faced, but Jack's features were set in a mask of determination. His revolver was still aimed straight at the corpse, utterly unwavering.

But the corpse seemed to accept, finally, that enough was enough. It sank to its knees with a series of dry cracks, shaking and twitching.

'It's over,' said Jack, although he kept the gun trained on the shattered remains of the skull as the cadaver started to waver.

Then, with a last, dry rasp of dead breath, the corpse collapsed. It lay on its back, cold and stiff once again, its face turned sightlessly up towards the glaring lights.

For a second everyone held their positions: Jack with his gun trained on the body, Owen standing by him, Gwen with her hands to her face. Above them, looking down in disbelieving horror, Toshiko and Ianto.

Sticky lumps of black blood dribbled down the tiles and, beneath the shattered skull, a huge mess of brain and bone sat in a thick puddle of blood.

'I'd just got this place spotless, too,' said Ianto.

TEN

'So what the hell happened there?' demanded Jack. He was circling the desk in his office, arms folded. 'I thought you said you were bringing a dead body in for examination. Didn't you think to check he actually was dead first?'

Gwen knew he was being sarcastic, but the tone still stung.

'Be fair, Jack,' said Owen from the doorway. 'Y'know, the guy had done a lot to make himself look dead: lain in a bog for forty years, decayed himself, let the worms in, shrivelled up a bit, stopped breathing, no circulation, all major organs dried up and inactive. Could've fooled anyone.'

'Thanks, Owen,' said Gwen acidly.

'OK, so he was dead,' Jack admitted, stalking past Owen. He looked down into the Autopsy Room. The corpse, now returned to the examination table, had been strapped down. 'It raises the question, though: why didn't he stay dead?'

'I've been thinking about that,' Gwen said. 'We know the corpse shows traces of Rift energy. It has a connection with the weak spot in time here.' She looked up and met Jack's gaze. 'Could it have anything to do with you?'

'What do you mean?'

'Being this close to the actual Rift.' Gwen flicked her gaze at the chromium pillar running through the centre of the Hub. 'Being this close to you – someone who cannot die.'

Jack held her gaze. 'Not buying it.'

'Why not? It only came back to life when it was here with you and the Rift! It showed nothing of that beforehand – not when we found it, not when we put it in the boot of my car, not when it was brought down here.'

Jack frowned. 'So why isn't it still alive now? Same Rift, same me.'

'Could be something to do with you blowing what was left of its brains all over the walls,' suggested Owen, and then he held up a hand. 'No, wait, sorry – that would still only be a clinical definition of something that had to be dead. It may not agree.'

'So what are we looking at here?' Jack wanted to know. 'A zombie?'

'Or a vampire?' Gwen said.

Owen sighed and dragged a hand down his face. He needed a shave. 'We can't rule anything out at this stage. Tosh is running some tests right now. Maybe she can come up with something.'

Jack turned back to look at the corpse on the table as Gwen joined him. 'It hasn't moved again,' she said. 'It looks exactly like what it is – a body that's lain dead in a bog for forty years.'

'Yeah,' said Jack with a cold smile, 'which is exactly what it looked like an hour ago, before it decided to make a bigger comeback than Frank Sinatra.' He watched Ianto moving around the Autopsy Room, carefully and methodically cleaning the place up, but making sure he kept well out of the corpse's reach.

'You'd better come and see this.' Toshiko was sitting at her workstation, her smooth features lit by the glare from the bank of computer screens mounted above the desk. Her fingers were already rattling across a number of keyboards, and various images flickered over the monitors in response.

'What you got for us, Tosh?' Jack leant over her desk and studied the screens. A couple of them showed images relayed from the Autopsy Room: the corpse strapped to the table, and an X-ray of the body. Others showed spectrographic analyses of various factors, and another was showing a digital recording of the moment when the corpse first moved.

On the screen, Owen leant over the body to make the first incision, and then suddenly reeled back as the corpse jerked into life.

'What's this then,' asked Owen, peering at the images, '*Dawn of the Dead* re-run?'

'Keep watching,' said Tosh.

They all watched the recording as the corpse climbed off the table, dragged Gwen down, and then took the first bullet from Jack's gun.

Gwen flinched as she watched, remembering the cold wetness speckling her face as the corpse lurched away from her.

On the screen, the dead body continued to struggle, knocking over the trolley and finally getting a sizeable part of the remains of its head removed by Jack's second shot. It sank to its knees and collapsed, dead, again.

'I've seen this before,' Jack said.

'Didn't like it much the first time,' said Gwen.

'Me neither,' Owen agreed. 'I hate repeats.'

'Wait,' said Toshiko, touching a control so that the image reversed rapidly to the moment when the corpse started moving. 'Listen carefully.'

'If you're saying someone farted,' said Owen, 'then I'm afraid it was me. Understandable, I think, in the circumstances.'

'No, listen,' said Toshiko, in no mood for jokes. 'You can only just hear it…'

She replayed the scene again, tweaking the volume. This time they could clearly hear the scrape of the corpse's movement, the startled yelp from Gwen as it grabbed her ankle and pulled. They watched as it drew her closer, Gwen recoiling, heard the sharp hiss of breath.

'It's saying something,' Jack realised.

'Probably couldn't speak very clearly anyway,' said Owen. 'No lips, jaws all stiff, tongue and larynx shrivelled up like leaves. Even if it was trying to say something, it wouldn't be able to articulate the words properly.'

'Something about rags?' suggested Gwen.

'Maybe we should ask him,' said Owen. 'Excuse me, but would you mind coming back to life again just one more time, we didn't quite catch what you said before.'

'Play it again,' said Jack.

They listened.

'Definitely "rags" or "rag",' said Gwen. 'I'm sure of it.'

'The "s" sound may not be correct,' Toshiko advised them. 'There are no lips or tongue to control the speech. It's trying to say something, but it hasn't got the means to do it properly.'

'Might as well be "gottle o' gear",' said Owen.

'Wait – the computer's found a match,' said Toshiko. She touched a control and the sound was replayed again, cleaned and stripped of all extraneous white noise. 'What if we play that back alongside the visual image?' She grabbed a keyboard and started typing. Within a few seconds, she had the original video image running again, this time with the enhanced audio.

The corpse slid off the autopsy table, grabbed Gwen, pulled her close. It looked at her, or tried to, and said, 'Water hag! Water hag!'

And then there was a series of distorted, muffled noises as Owen and Jack spoke on the tape and Jack's revolver had the last word.

ELEVEN

Bob Strong woke up with a coughing fit. He had fallen asleep on the sofa again, but he couldn't manage more than a few minutes dozing before the next spasm came. If he had the flu, then he was going to go through hell, he knew that. So many people called a bad cold 'flu', but as a doctor he knew there was a vast difference between the common cold and influenza. He knew he could look forward to severe headaches, body cramps, fever, even delirium.

He popped some heavy-duty painkillers down and a decongestant, although they didn't seem to be having much of an effect. Every time he coughed, he felt as if his chest and throat were on fire as he brought up more burning phlegm, and the reverberations sent shockwaves through his brain.

He lay on the sofa and sweated his way through *Richard & Judy*. It crossed his mind to get a flu jab – it might just hold off the worst of it, he thought. But in truth he felt too ill to move and there was no way he could get to the surgery. He tried to phone Iuean Evans, but each time he dialled the surgery the line was busy. Then he tried Iuean's mobile, but that was either switched off or on silent, because he wasn't answering. Eventually the phone slipped out of Bob's fingers because they were so sweaty, and he couldn't be bothered leaning down to pick it up off the floor.

He watched all of *Scrum V* through a daze, coughing and retching painfully. In one particularly bad fit, he found his tissue speckled with red and green matter. He was coughing so hard his throat was raw. He slumped back into the cushions with a groan. His head was pounding. The rumble of traffic outside his window seemed to shake the entire house as if an express train was running past continuously.

Eventually, he heard his mobile phone ringing. He fumbled around with one hand beneath the sofa, picked up the phone and flipped it open. 'Iuean?'

'Bob, how's it going?' boomed the familiar voice.

'Bloody awful. I feel like hell.' He broke off to cough again, bringing up more phlegm striped with red. 'Oh, God, sorry… I don't think I'm gonna be in for the rest of the week, Iuean.'

'Bob, we need you here,' said Iuean. His voice sounded strained. 'It's absolute bedlam! They've been coming in bloody droves. Chest infections, coughs, flu, whatever you want to call it. Nothing adds up, but they just keep coming. We've had to turn some away. We've redirected them to Blackweir. One or two I sent direct to St Helen's.'

Bob struggled to sit up. 'Hell, Iuean, I'm sorry. I didn't think it was that bad. Sounds like they've got what I've got.'

'So what are we looking at here? An epidemic?'

'Have you checked with the surrounding practices?'

'I wanted to talk to you first. I've already had someone from the local press sniffing round.'

'OK.' Bob paused to cough again. 'You'll have to keep accurate records of how many patients come in with flu symptoms.'

'Yes, I know that. I've already got Letty on it. We can only declare it an epidemic if 400 people per 100,000 of the population are diagnosed.'

'I don't think it'll get that far,' Bob assured him.

'So what do you think it is?'

'Iuean, I haven't the foggiest!' Bob thought for a moment about telling Iuean about his visit from Owen Harper. But Iuean sounded genuinely worried, and Bob feared that the involvement of a government official taking blood samples would only alarm him further. Harper had said it was only precautionary, but it was still confidential. And, at the end of the day, it could all just be a local phenomenon. 'It's probably a virus or something, anyway,' he said weakly.

'Well, that is what we tell people when we don't know what's bloody wrong with them.'

'Look, give me tonight. Let's see how I am in the morning. If I can, I'll come in.'

'No, stay where you are. You sound rough. You need to get better. We can manage. If necessary I'll bring a locum in and we'll get by. I just hope this was the worst of it today.'

'Thanks, mate.' Bob dissolved into more coughs and closed the phone. He felt sorry for Iuean, but he really was in too bad a way to go into work again. He fell back on the sofa, eyes squeezed shut, coughing and holding his chest as if it was about to crack open.

'What if it wasn't attacking us?' said Toshiko.

'Mr Dead down there was trying to strangle Gwen, in case

you hadn't noticed,' responded Owen. 'In my book, that constitutes an attack.'

'But was he?' asked Toshiko. She looked at each of them in turn. 'Attacking her, I mean. You've all seen the footage. He grabbed her, certainly. Pulled her down from the steps. But what then?'

'I thought he was gonna kiss her,' said Jack. He shrugged. 'Well, I would've.'

'I'm not that kind of girl,' said Gwen with a weak smile. 'I mean, I don't date corpses as a rule.'

'What about Rhys?' asked Owen.

Gwen gave him two fingers without even looking.

'I thought it was trying to see her,' continued Toshiko. 'Its eyes were all shrivelled up and gone, but it was going through the motions, almost trying to peer at her...'

Jack clicked his fingers. 'And then it says "water hag", right?'

'Twice, so far as we can tell. Or something very like it.'

Jack leant against Toshiko's workstation with a frown, lips pursed, considering.

'Maybe he mistook Gwen for some old hag,' Owen suggested. When Gwen narrowed her eyes at him, he added, 'No, seriously... the first thing he does when he wakes up after forty years dead is roll off the autopsy table and see Gwen. Or, at least, a blurred version of Gwen. He certainly wouldn't have been able to see her clearly. But maybe he could tell she was a woman – small, long hair. That would be enough.'

'But a hag?' Gwen repeated. 'Thanks very much.'

'We don't know what the last thing he saw before he died was, do we?' Owen said. 'Maybe it was some evil old witch with a knife.'

'Thanks.'

'Or maybe,' said Toshiko, 'he was trying to warn us about Sally Blackteeth.'

Owen frowned. 'Who?'

'Professor Len used the term "water hag", I'm sure of it,' Toshiko said. 'He was telling us about the local legends surrounding Greendown Moss. Evil spirits who live in stagnant water.'

'It's worth checking,' Gwen said. 'I'll contact the professor and see what he says.'

'It still won't tell us what brought the corpse back to life, though,' Toshiko said.

'That's assuming he was really dead,' said Jack.

'As opposed to just pretending for forty years.'

'Hang on,' Owen raised a hand. 'When did "it" become "he", please?'

'Well, you did say the body was male,' Toshiko said.

'It is.'

'And we don't have a name, do we?'

'No.'

'So it doesn't seem fair to carry on referring to him as an "it".' Toshiko stared at them. 'In my opinion.'

'That's all right for you to say,' Gwen replied. 'It wasn't you he was leering at.' She shuddered and reached for her coffee. 'I can still smell that thing's breath.'

'I'm just saying, that's all,' Toshiko protested. 'We can't be certain of anything, can we?'

'We can't even be certain it's properly dead this time,' Owen agreed. 'I'd have placed bets on it before. Now, I'm not so sure. Anyone want to give me odds?'

'Owen, half its head's missing now.'

'Lengthens the odds a bit, I'll agree, but…'

'We need to know exactly what reanimated that body,' announced Jack, standing up. 'Any ideas before I let Owen loose on it again?'

'I don't mind going in with the knife, so long as someone else holds it down,' Owen said.

'Won't be necessary. Ianto's strapped it down. It's secure.'

'All right, but just for the record I think I should tell you I'm not happy carrying out an autopsy on a patient that needs restraining while I do it.'

'Everyone!' Ianto's voice came up from the Autopsy Room, sounding urgent. 'You'd better get down here quick!'

Owen dodged past Jack and took the stairs three at a time. Jack clattered after him, with Toshiko and Gwen on his heels. 'It better not be coming back to life again,' Jack warned. 'It's getting kinda personal now!'

Ianto, a bucket by his feet and a pair of rubber gloves on, was pointing at the corpse.

The body was still on the table, securely strapped down. It wasn't going anywhere, and neither did it appear to be moving.

'What's up, Ianto?' asked Jack, loosening the flap on his holster.

Gwen circled the table warily, not wanting to look too closely at the gaping hole in the top of the brown skull. One glance was enough to tell her that it was only half-full of dried brain matter.

'I saw it move,' said Ianto.

'Again?' said Jack.

'Looks OK to me,' Owen remarked. 'I mean, for a guy who's

died twice already. How much deader can he get?'

'So it's a "he" now, is it?' queried Ianto.

'Look!' Toshiko said, pointing.

They looked. The body twitched.

'There you are,' said Ianto with a nod of satisfaction. 'I said I saw it move.'

Jack drew his revolver, and this time Gwen had her automatic in both hands as well.

The corpse twitched and shuddered again, as if a tremor was running through its emaciated torso.

'What's going on?' Jack demanded. 'Some kind of nerve impulse?'

'Death throes?' Owen shook his head. 'Bit late for that.'

Toshiko, scientific curiosity overcoming her instinctive fear, leant in for a closer look, running one of her hand-held scanners over the body.

'Careful, Tosh,' Gwen warned, moving into a slightly better line of sight.

'It's not the corpse moving,' Toshiko said quietly. 'I mean, it's only moving because something else is moving it... Something inside.'

Suddenly there was a muffled crack from the corpse's chest area, and Toshiko jerked backwards. Jack raised his pistol and aimed, Gwen mirroring the movement next to him.

The corpse wriggled again and now, after what Toshiko had said, they could see that it was being moved by something else.

'There is something inside it,' realised Owen. 'Something moving...'

Gwen tightened her grip on the automatic. 'What? What is it?'

'Giant maggot?' Owen wondered.

Then the corpse's throat bulged and its mouth opened. The shattered skull began to shake as something forced its way out between the bared teeth like a giant tongue.

It was dark and glistening, coated in thick, congealed blood like a piece of raw liver. The jaws opened wider, accompanied by the dull crack of snapping bone and stiffened ligaments, as the thing extruded itself like a huge slug.

The skull finally cracked wide open then, revealing a foetal shape nestling in the remains of the jaws and throat, covered by a web of sticky mucous. The shape moved, flexing, opening like a moth emerging from its chrysalis, stretching out spindly, insect-like limbs.

'Oh my God,' said Gwen, her voice quavering. 'It's... human.'

A tiny head turned to look at her. Beneath the clotted slime of blood, two eyes glared out and a vicious slit of a mouth opened in a mewling hiss.

Then a gunshot boomed out, heavy and final, and the newborn creature exploded into bloody fragments.

Jack and Gwen turned to look at Owen, who had his own gun out, the barrel smoking. He was still aiming at the remains, his face twisted into a mask of utter revulsion.

'What did you shoot it for?' asked Jack.

'Didn't you see it?' asked Owen, half-choking. 'Did you see what it looked like? It was...'

'Human?' Gwen repeated.

'No.' Owen shook his head. 'No, no, no. It was not human.'

'Alien, then,' said Jack, firmly. 'Do we shoot aliens on sight now, Owen?'

Slowly Owen lowered the gun and looked at the ground, He wouldn't meet the gaze of his colleagues. 'It wasn't right. It was… it wasn't right.' And then, without another word, he turned and left the room.

Toshiko was already investigating the remains of the creature. 'It must have been alive in there all the time,' she said, indicating the corpse. 'Incubated, perhaps…'

'By a corpse?'

'Why not? Flies are.'

'That thing wasn't a fly,' said Gwen.

'Whatever it was, I want to know,' Jack told Toshiko. 'Piece it back together if you have to, we need to find out exactly what it was. Work with Owen.'

'Owen?'

Jack nodded, heading for the exit. 'I'll sort him out now.'

'No, let me,' said Gwen, putting a hand on his arm. 'I'll see him.'

TWELVE

Bob was struggling to breathe. He felt as if his throat had swollen so much it was closing off his larynx. He jerked awake from his half-sleep, caught in a panic because he couldn't breathe. Couldn't breathe. Every basic instinct to inhale had somehow been forgotten.

He catapulted himself off the sofa and landed awkwardly on the floor, half-kneeling, retching and gagging. Eventually, he managed to suck in a lungful of air and then blow it back out. He could feel his heart hammering in the chest as he did so, straining to carry enough oxygen around his body. He wheezed and groaned for two more minutes until he felt able to sit back and congratulate himself on still being alive.

He'd treated people before with sleep-related breathing disorders – a strange condition where the body simply stopped breathing, usually when asleep, in the middle of the night. Often the condition was relieved by simply turning over, or waking up, and breathing resumed as normal. In research, some patients had been recorded as having stopped breathing for a full thirty to sixty seconds before recommencing.

He'd never experienced it himself, and it was terrifying. More terrifying than the sore throat and agonising cough that had accompanied his day so far. The basic need to breathe, to oxygenate the body and the brain, was at the core of every living being. Denied that ability, panic set in with astonishing speed. You could go without food or drink for days. Without oxygen you wouldn't last more than a couple of minutes.

Bob picked himself up off the floor and headed for the bathroom, coughing and retching. He felt sick and exhausted. As he climbed the stairs, he found bright spots of light flaring in his vision. When he reached the bathroom, he looked in the mirror and nearly collapsed there and then.

The man in the glass didn't look anything like Bob Strong. He was gaunt, grey-skinned, dark circles under red-rimmed eyes. There was still a trace of cyanosis around his lips. He really had been asleep without breathing, and for some time. He rubbed the cold skin of his face, trying to bring a bit of colour – the right colour – back to his complexion.

He coughed again, speckling the white sink with red and green blobs.

'Oh, God,' he groaned. 'When is this going to stop…?'

He walked slowly back downstairs to the living room. The traffic went by outside his window, people walking past on their way, oblivious to the plight he was in. In times gone by, his wife would have been there for him. She'd have fetched him blankets, tea, all that. She would have moaned about it, and complained that all men were such babies when it came to being ill, but she had been good at caring for people. Right now, Bob had never felt so alone, and he desperately wanted to speak to her again. And she would have found that so typical – that he only thought to contact her again when he was sick.

He picked up the phone and then sank down into the sofa, hunched over as he coughed again. Her mobile number was on speed dial, but what would be the point of phoning her now? She wouldn't come round to see him. She might catch whatever he had, anyway. But maybe it would be nice just to hear her voice. Anyone's voice.

He physically jumped when the telephone rang in his hand.

'Hello?'

'Bob, how are you, dear?'

Bob gripped the phone tighter. 'Mum? What are you doing ringing now?'

'Well, I wanted to know if you were coming up for your Dad's birthday or not. He's eighty next month, remember, and we're planning a party. Everyone will be there. I rang you at the surgery but they said you'd gone home poorly. What's the matter?'

'I don't know,' Bob said. 'Some sort of throat infection I think. I'm not sure.'

'It's not anything to do with what's been on the news, is it? That sounds awful.'

'What's been on the news?'

'The flu epidemic in Wales. It's in your region, dear.'

'I hadn't heard,' Bob said. He felt a surge of anxiety and fumbled for the TV remote as his mother continued to talk.

'Have you taken anything for it? Have you made yourself a hot drink? I always used to make you a lemon and honey drink, do you remember?' She spoke so warmly; she had never stopped thinking of Bob as her youngest boy and, whenever he was ill or unhappy, she adopted the same tone she had used when treating a grazed knee or a nosebleed when he had been little. 'Are you eating properly? Would you like me to come over? Perhaps I could help…'

'Mum, I'm thirty-eight. I don't need to be looked after.' He said this more harshly than he'd intended, and the silence at the other end of the line told him it had been noted. 'Look, I'm sorry, I'm just feeling really rough right now. It's not a good time.'

'That's why someone should come round,' his mother said, relenting a little. 'You need looking after, Bob. I always said so. Men can never look after themselves properly when they're ill.'

'No, really.' Bob's parents had moved up from Richmond to live in Hereford last year. It had been a big move for them at their age, but Robert Strong Senior was frailer than he liked to admit, and the bungalow had seemed like a good idea. His mother had come from Herefordshire originally, and she had always wanted to move back there, away from London. And Bob was not unaware of the fact that it brought both his parents that bit closer to where he now lived in Cardiff. It was only an hour's drive from his own house to their new bungalow, and he realised now that he had not visited as often as he had originally said he would – and certainly not as often as he should.

'How is Dad?' Bob asked eventually, after another coughing fit.

'He's doing very well,' came the reply, although judging by the tone, not as well as Mum had hoped. 'He still finds walking difficult, and of course he can't get up from his chair, poor dear.'

Bob heard another voice call out from in the room. 'What was that?'

'That was your father interrupting, dear. He said whatever you do, don't grow old…'

'It's rubbish!' Dad's voice piped up from the far side of the living room.

'Tell him he's doing OK,' Bob said, 'And I'll consider myself lucky if I get anywhere near his age.'

He listened to his mother recounting this and heard a muffled reply from his father. Bob squeezed his eyes shut and felt his throat stiffening. Suddenly, more than anything, he wanted to see his parents again. 'And tell him I'll be there for his birthday,' he added thickly. 'In fact, as soon as I'm feeling better, I'll come and visit.'

There was a definite lift in his mother's voice now. 'Perhaps you could stay over, even if it's just for one night. That would be lovely.'

'Yeah, I'd like that. I'll come for a weekend.'

'That's lovely. Tell me when you're coming and I'll make sure I've got plenty in. Your father doesn't eat much these days – he's only having chicken soup for his dinner now – and I've got to be careful, so I'll buy in specially.'

'Great.'

'And get better soon. You sound awful.'

'OK, Mum. Thanks.'

'I'll call you again tomorrow. Take care, love.'

'Yeah. Love you. Bye.'

Bob switched the phone off and sank back into the cushions. He coughed up a mouthful of thick, stinking phlegm and spat it into a tissue. The urge to vomit was becoming increasing difficult to ignore.

He switched the TV back on to distract him. There was a programme about estate agents on one channel, and on another it was beeswax. He flicked to another channel and this time picked up a news bulletin.

The so-called flu epidemic had indeed made the news. Certainly there was a mention of it midway through the second round-up, as reports came in from across the UK of a sharp increase in respiratory complaints. Bob sat up at this point and listened properly.

'... and a spokesperson for the Ministry of Health said it was too early to say whether or not this represented a serious flu epidemic.'

The picture switched to a junior health minister – Bob didn't bother looking at the name which scrolled along the bottom of the screen – standing in front of the Houses of Parliament saying, 'We don't want to overreact to this, obviously. The National Health Service has every provision in place to not only recognise a serious epidemic, but to cope with it as well. So far we have not had to reach that stage, and I don't think we will.'

The picture changed back to a shot of a doctor's surgery somewhere. 'Nevertheless, many GPs are concerned at the sudden increase in respiratory problems, which, they said, cannot entirely be blamed on seasonal variations.'

Cut to a GP in his surgery, an older guy, wearing heavy glasses. The caption said Dr Graham Walker. 'I've seen nearly four to five times as many patients in the last week with what I would term serious respiratory conditions. It isn't normal, and we should be on our guard. The problem is that Westminster is ignoring this simply because the epidemic is in Wales and not London.'

'Some commentators feel that the concerns of GPs are being overlooked, and this may be putting the public's health at risk,' the reporter continued. 'The Government has been quick to point out, however, that there is a widespread vaccination programme available for free for anyone over sixty-five to protect against flu. This is also true for vulnerable people below that age, such as those with chronic heart disease, diabetes, kidney disease or asthma sufferers. This is David Coulton, reporting for BBC News 24.'

Bob muted the TV and coughed into his tissue again. A part of him felt just a little bit better knowing that he was not the only person suffering, but he did wonder what, if anything, the Government would do. Perhaps nothing until his blood sample had been checked.

THIRTEEN

Gwen eventually found Owen standing at the rail at Mermaid Quay. It was chilly so close to the water, and she had to pull her denim jacket tighter to ward off the hard south-easterly blowing in towards Cardiff. Owen was still in a T-shirt, looking out across the bay.

'Hey,' Gwen said as she joined him at the rail.

'Don't bother,' muttered Owen, without taking his eyes off the horizon.

'Don't bother what?'

'Don't bother trying to sweet-talk me back into the Hub. I need a break.'

'We're all pretty tired,' Gwen remarked evenly. 'Jack says he needs you though.'

That provoked a harsh laugh. 'Sent you up after me, did he? Thought you could work your womanly wiles and get me to come running back? So I can go back in and say sorry I messed up, Jack. Again. Please let me prove myself to you by solving the problem in five minutes flat.'

'Bollocks,' said Gwen. 'It's not like that and you know it. Jack wanted to come after you himself.'

'That would've been even worse.'

'I said I'd come because I knew how you'd be feeling.'

He looked at her for the first time. 'Bet you don't.'

'Yeah, I do. You're feeling pretty stupid and ashamed for reacting like that. Not only did you mess up and overreact, you shot our only chance of finding out what this is all about.'

'It wasn't human.'

'Maybe not – but it was humanoid.'

'Doesn't mean it didn't need shooting. I can think of quite a few humanoids and humans I know who could do with shooting.'

'Says Dr Owen Harper.'

A slight smirk. 'You really want to know why I pulled the trigger?'

She shrugged. 'I think you just freaked because it looked like a tiny little person. A baby.'

'No. It wasn't me who freaked. I pulled the trigger 'cos I knew you lot wouldn't.' Owen turned around so his back was to the bay, folded his arms and leant against the rail. 'Jack always holds back – he likes to give the benefit of the doubt and you wouldn't shoot because... well, because it looked like an infant.'

Gwen flinched. 'What do you mean?'

'It was small, newborn, looked a bit helpless,' Owen said matter-of-factly. 'Classic infant survival technique. The maternal instinct in you wouldn't allow you to shoot.'

'Is that so wrong?'

Now Owen turned to look at her, staring straight into

her eyes. 'That wasn't a baby, Gwen. It didn't even look like a baby.'

'OK. So what was it?'

'I dunno, yet.'

'So why'd you shoot it?'

'Because I could tell – I could feel it – the way it looked, the way it sounded. It was all wrong. Unnatural.'

Gwen took a deep breath, pulling her hair away from her face as the bay wind flapped it around her head. 'Well, it's dead now. So you can come back, take a proper look. Maybe come up with something a bit more useful than "unnatural". That's what we deal with every day, isn't it?'

'Yeah. But this was… something else. I can't explain it. It was just instinct.'

'Well, now your instincts should tell you that we need to find out what it was, and try to explain it.' She touched him on the arm. 'What's done is done, Owen. You shot it. It's dead. Let's move on.'

'May as well,' Owen grunted. He hunched up his shoulders. 'Besides, it's freezing out here.'

Toshiko, wearing surgical gloves, placed what remained of the creature on a tray. The bullet had blown it into fragments, but, picking up what looked like pieces of hardened mucus she'd found on the floor of the Autopsy Room, she had been able to complete part of the jigsaw. She had a surgical mask over her nose and mouth to keep out the stench. Ianto had already complained that it had filled the room with a smell like a compost heap.

'What are you going to do?' Jack asked as he watched Toshiko work, his face stony with distaste as the putrid smell

121

reached his nose. 'Sew the pieces back together and run a couple of thousand volts through it?'

Toshiko gave him a cool look and then returned to her examination.

The creature would have been about eighteen inches high when stretched out. It was humanoid, with a tough, fibrous green skin. The head had been completely disintegrated by Owen's shot, so there was no way of seeing that properly again, but there had been scraps of the weed-like substance left. Toshiko put them on slides and checked them out under a microscope along with strips of flesh.

'This is quite extraordinary,' she said, looking up over the top of her glasses at Jack. 'I've made a chemical analysis of the flesh. It's actually a hardened slime made up from various inorganic salts, desquamated cells and leucocytes. In other words, it appears to be made primarily from mucus.'

'S'not very nice.'

'There are traces of vegetable matter here, too, though,' Toshiko reported thoughtfully. 'Actually part of the flesh.'

'You mean it could be a vegetable life form?' Jack didn't seem amazed by this. It was a genuine query. Sometimes the depth of his knowledge about alien life still took Toshiko by surprise.

'No,' she replied. 'I'm not sure. It's neither plant nor animal nor wholly mucoid; just a bit of everything. It would explain the smell, though – bacteria at work in rotting vegetation.'

Jack was staring at the remains with a deep frown on his otherwise smooth features, and Toshiko noticed when she looked up. 'It's kind of familiar,' he said quietly, in response to her quizzical look.

'The smell?'

'No. The look of it. Reminds me of something…' Jack still seemed to be turning it over in his mind, as if he was sorting through a hundred thousand different experiences, searching for a tiny scrap of useful information. He approached the examination tray and reached out towards the remains, but he made sure he didn't touch it. His lips parted slightly, and then he said, 'Homunculus.'

'Latin, meaning literally, "little man" or "manikin",' said Toshiko, nodding. 'I see what you mean.'

'There's something about it,' mused Jack, as if he hadn't heard her. 'Something at the back of my mind. That word – *homunculus* – I dunno why, but it just fits. I know it does.'

'Something you remember?'

'Wish I could.'

'Relax. It'll come to you.' Toshiko smiled at him. 'You need a rest.'

Jack ran a hand through his hair and said, 'What I need is more coffee. Ianto!'

'A man's work is never done in Torchwood,' said Ianto, peeling off his rubber gloves. 'If you want coffee on demand, you'll have to stop mucking the place up first.'

'Get to it before I put you over my knee.' Jack grinned at him and turned back to Toshiko. 'Tosh, what was this thing doing inside that corpse? How'd it get in there?'

'I think our original idea was close to the truth,' she replied. 'It had been growing in there. I don't think it had reached full maturity, but it was clearly ready to emerge – I'm wondering if it may have been responsible for keeping the corpse in a state of suspended animation for the last forty years in the marsh.'

'And that's why it suddenly woke up?'

'Well, there's still plenty of chronon discharge registering, but it's still a more likely explanation than some kind of fallout from the Rift.'

'OK, I'll buy that. Still don't know what it is, though.'

'Homunculus?'

Jack shrugged. 'I'm working on it.'

There was a clatter of footsteps on the flooring, and they looked up to see Owen approaching. He was trying to conceal his sheepishness behind an arrogant façade, and almost – but not quite – failing.

'I know, I know,' he said, holding up his hands. 'Don't all rush to hug me, you'll only embarrass me.'

'Hug you?' queried Jack. 'Hey, even I have standards.'

'Thank you, Captain.' Owen raised both eyebrows in a look of pure innocence that almost – but not quite – succeeded. 'Anyway, back now, sulk over. What's next?'

'Tosh has been examining what's left of the…'

'The…?'

'The whatever-it-is.'

'Ugly-looking thing, isn't it?' said Owen. 'The whatever-it-is ain't much better either.' He flashed a grin at Toshiko and winked. 'You know I'm only joking.'

'I think it's some kind of infant,' Toshiko said shortly.

'I've already had this conversation. That's no baby, Tosh.' He leant over her to examine the readings on the monitor and raised his eyebrows. 'For one thing it's made out of snot, according to this.'

'And by infant I mean it may not be fully grown.' Toshiko indicated the series of computer analysis screens by her workstation. 'Look at these molecular spectroscopy readings. The concentration levels are incredible. It's like there's so much energy contained within each cell, just waiting for a release.'

'Any chance of that happening now?' asked Jack warily.

'No. It's dead, not dormant.'

'Good job I shot it, then,' said Owen.

Jack paced around the workstation thoughtfully. 'So we have a dead body acting as an incubator for this thing, lying at the bottom of a peat bog for over forty years until Tosh found it.'

'Lucky old me,' said Toshiko.

Gwen approached the huddle with a sheaf of paperwork in her hand. 'I've done some research on water hags,' she announced. 'I did try phoning Professor Len, but he's not picking up.'

Toshiko smiled. 'Pity. I liked him.'

'Well, he did save your life.'

'That always does it for me.'

Owen looked up. 'So you typed "water hag" into Google and pressed enter. I don't know… With all your police training and dedication to duty I'd have expected more. Whatever happened to the plod's meticulous fact-finding and slow-but-sure attitude? I think you could have gone that extra mile and tried Wikipedia.'

'You're so funny, Owen,' Gwen said without a trace of a smile. She held up the hard copy for Jack and Toshiko to see. 'Thought I'd print it off rather than send it across.'

'Surprised you didn't write it all down in your little notebook,' muttered Owen.

Gwen ignored him. 'Water hags are basically lumps of marsh weed that look vaguely like an old woman lurking underwater,' she said. 'That's the fact side of things, anyway.

125

They were commonly sighted in medieval times in areas of marshland all over the country, but they sort of went out of superstition fashion a long time ago. There are some references in literature and folklore down through the ages, though, and famously there was a giant water hag in *Beowulf*. She was Grendel's mother, and she used to live under a black lake and drag people down to their deaths with hooked talons.'

'I think I went out with her once,' said Owen.

'Which is probably why Beowulf killed her with his magic sword,' Gwen said. 'Put the poor woman out of her misery.'

'Ho, ho, ho.'

'There was another well-known water hag in Cheshire called Jenny Greenteeth,' Gwen continued. 'She used to lurk in ditches and drag unwary travellers down to her underwater den.'

'Jenny Greenteeth?' repeated Owen. 'Yep, definitely went out with her.'

'Professor Len said that some of these water spirits could disguise themselves as normal women,' Toshiko said.

'There you are then.'

'The point is,' said Gwen, 'it's all the same kind of location and the same modus operandi.'

'So Professor Len was right after all,' said Toshiko.

'You reckon our dead friend back there was an unwary traveller?' wondered Jack, jabbing a thumb towards the Autopsy Room. 'Walking across the Greendown Moss one night forty years back, and dragged down by one of these old witches?'

'Sally Blackteeth, to be precise,' said Toshiko. 'That's the name of the water hag Professor Len told us about.'

'And there's something else which may be relevant,' said Gwen. 'These witches or water hags couldn't have children. They dragged men down into the swamp but it never worked out. So they used to make their own children out of dried snot and mud.'

'The homunculus,' said Toshiko quietly.

There was silence for a moment before Owen said, 'But if these water hag things went off the superstition radar like you say, what's brought them back again now?'

'Well, in the absence of Professor Len, I did go that extra mile,' Gwen smiled sweetly, 'and came up with this.' She placed a sheet of paper on Toshiko's desk. 'Several more water hag sightings in modern times. They're not as old-fashioned as you think.'

Jack picked up the hard copy and scanned it. 'Nine sightings in the last year alone. Why didn't we spot this sooner?'

'We're on the lookout for all sorts of things,' Toshiko argued. 'We can't follow up every single paranormal sighting or report.'

'But look at the locations,' said Jack, snapping his fingers against the paper. 'Six of these were within a five-mile radius of here.'

They all knew what he meant by that – the chromium tower rising through the centre of the Hub, trickling with water, the base practically covered in moss and algae.

'The Rift,' nodded Toshiko, moving around so that she could check the report herself. 'We know these things have a special connection with space-time – and I've correlated chronon discharges with nearly all of these areas. If I made a closer comparison, I bet they'd be exact matches.'

'Get on it – double-check. We need to know for sure.' Jack

tossed the papers towards Gwen and Owen, adding, 'Look – there was even one sighted in the local canal! Right under our noses.'

'Anywhere there are stagnant ponds or marshy areas,' Gwen said, studying the map. 'Even in city areas.'

There was a polite cough from behind them. When they looked around, they saw Ianto standing a little off to the side. 'I can only think it appropriate at this point to remind you about Saskia Harden,' he said.

'Who?' Jack frowned.

Owen straightened up, saying, 'The girl I went to Trynsel to investigate…?'

'The serial suicide?'

Ianto nodded. 'That's right. If you recall, she had been found by the police floating in water, on a number of occasions. In a canal, in a pond, in a disused swimming pool…'

'Stagnant water,' said Toshiko. 'Or as near as she could find.'

'Could she be a water hag?' wondered Gwen.

'Let's ask her,' said Jack. He turned to Owen, only to find him already heading for the exit.

FOURTEEN

Owen drove straight to Bob Strong's house. He felt vaguely guilty for not having taken Ianto's original request seriously enough, but Strong's illness had seemed more important at the time and Owen had forgotten all about Saskia Harden.

He was reminded of just how bad Bob Strong was as soon as the door opened. His skin was grey-green and his eyes, beneath the heavy, swollen lids, were veined with blood.

Strong stood in the doorway for a moment, focusing. 'Oh, it's you,' he said gruffly. He coughed and then stood back. 'You'd better come in. Hope you've got some good news.'

As he spoke, he started coughing again and his knees buckled. Instinctively, Owen caught him, took his weight and helped him back inside the house.

'It's OK, it's OK,' Strong assured him, leaning on the furniture for support but making sure he took the shortest route back to the sofa. The room was a mess, full of half-drunk cups of coffee, medicine bottles, crumpled tissues and a terrible smell.

Owen sniffed cautiously. He knew what the smell was – sickness, illness. And something else. It took him a moment to work it out: rotten cabbages. Maybe something in the kitchen was going off.

Strong's cough sounded ragged and guttural, and Owen heard him moan as the pain ripped through his chest.

'Sit down,' Owen said. 'I'll get you something.'

'Feel… like… hell…' groaned Strong, lowering himself into the cushions of the settee.

'What have you taken?'

Strong's eyes were closing, as if he was too weak to reply.

'What have you taken?' Owen repeated, quickly sorting through the bottles of painkillers and decongestants spread across the floor. There was nothing too serious here.

'Found anything?' Strong asked.

'What?'

'The blood tests. What did they show?'

'Nothing,' Owen said truthfully. 'All clear.'

Strong was frowning now. 'I don't understand.'

'It's true. You're the picture of health, according to your blood tests, mate.'

'Feels like I'm gonna die,' said Strong. There had been, for a moment, a fleeting expression of relief on his face, but it was quickly displaced by a look of bewilderment and fear. 'So what the hell's wrong with me?'

Owen picked up his wrist and checked the pulse. He counted the beats off against the second hand on his watch. The heart rate was fast but steady. 'You're not going to die yet,' Owen told him. He prised open one of the puffy eyelids and looked at the eye beneath, producing a slim pencil torch from his jacket pocket to help.

The eyes looked sore but the pupils contracted when he shone the penlight at them.

'Open wide, Bob,' Owen said, turning the man's face towards him. 'I need to have a look at your throat, mate.'

The mouth duly opened, and, using a pencil as a makeshift tongue suppressor, Owen shone the torch into the man's throat.

It looked red and inflamed, which was what he expected. But there was something else there. Across the wet skin at the back of the mouth were a number of white sores, almost like mouth ulcers, some of them speckled with blood. There was a layer of foul-smelling mucus there too. So far so bad throat infection.

Then something moved at the back of Strong's throat.

Owen blinked, hardly believing it. He kept very still and shone the torch steadily at the soft flesh.

There it was again: a tiny movement, beneath the skin. The pink flesh rippled slightly as something squirmed under the surface.

Owen clicked off the torch. 'OK, close up. Nothing happening here.'

Strong swallowed with difficulty. 'What is it?'

'Too early to tell.'

'That's what you said last time.' Bob suddenly started coughing again, and Owen jerked back, not knowing what to expect but nevertheless wary.

'You been near any ponds recently? Canals? Stagnant water of any kind?'

'Don't think so. No. Why?'

'Do you know Saskia Harden?'

'Sorry?' Now Strong sat up, coughing abruptly, a querulous

look replacing the worried frown. 'Saskia Harden? What's she got to do with anything? How do you know her?'

'I don't,' Owen said. 'But you obviously do.'

Strong swallowed painfully again. 'Is she connected with this? Is she carrying something? A virus?'

'It's possible. We really need to talk to her.'

'You'd have to check the records at the medical centre.'

'We already have. The address on her file doesn't exist.' Owen saw Bob frowning and carried on, pressing home the questions. 'Do you have any idea where she might be? How we could find her?'

'Wait a minute. I... I saw her yesterday. In surgery. She came to see me. She's not been well – mental problems, that kind of thing. Some attempts at suicide. I don't know her all that well, but she...' Once again the words disappeared under a series of coughs. Strong grabbed a handkerchief, but not before he'd had to bring up an odious lump of green and red matter. 'Oh, God, I don't know how long I can take this,' he gasped. 'What's wrong with me? I should be in hospital, surely...'

Owen shook his head. 'No. Definitely no hospitals. Not yet. I don't want you taking this into a hospital, not until we know exactly what it is.'

'But they'll have facilities,' Strong argued. 'Quarantine.'

'This may not be something they would know how to deal with,' Owen warned.

'They have facilities for this sort of thing—'

'It's unlikely. No hospitals, not yet.' Owen stood up, signalling that the subject was closed. 'Is there anyone else at the medical centre who might know how to find Saskia Harden?'

Strong shook his head. 'No one. All we know is what's on the records.'

'OK. Sit tight.' Owen stood up, speed-dialling his mobile phone. 'Ianto? I can't trace Saskia from here. You're gonna have to find her yourself. Go back to the police records. See if there are any clues there. If you don't find anything, go back and check again. And get Gwen to help you – she's got a cop's instincts.'

'Gwen's gone out with Jack,' said Ianto.

'What for?'

'There's been a sighting – a water hag, we think. In Garron Park.'

'I'm on my way,' Owen snapped the phone shut and turned back to Strong. 'If you think of anything, anything at all, that might help us find Saskia Harden, ring me on this number.' He jotted something down on a piece of notepaper and handed it over.

'OK.' Bob glanced at the number and then folded it and slipped it into his shirt pocket.

Owen paused, raising a hand to rub at his neck. He swallowed, wincing a little.

'What's up?'

Owen shrugged and headed for the door. 'Nothing. Just getting a bit of a sore throat, I think.'

FIFTEEN

Jack and Gwen were in the SUV, hurtling through the streets of Cardiff. Jack was at the wheel, Gwen sat in the passenger seat, loading a fresh magazine into her automatic. Jack's eyes never left the road but he was still talking.

'I don't like this,' he said, biting the words off. 'I don't like running after something when I don't even know what it is.'

'The sighting was yesterday,' Gwen said. 'We have to follow it up.'

'The sighting was unconfirmed. It's internet chatter. An old woman lurking near the lake in Garron Park? Give me a break.'

'Then why are we speeding there like our lives depend on it?' asked Gwen.

'May be I'm just tired of waiting around.'

Jack swung the SUV into a tight bend, the street lamps painting stripes of orange across his face as the car roared along the avenue. 'Anyway,' he went on, 'Tosh says there's a pattern of Rift activity centring on the park. Rift sparks.

Best place in the city to find the kind of water these creatures like.'

The SUV skidded to a halt by the park gates, and they scrambled out. Jack flipped open his leather wrist-strap and checked the readings. A green light flickered on the display and it beeped metronomically. 'Chronon discharge – this way,' he said, starting towards the park gates.

The main paths through the park were lit, but it was deserted and some areas were in total darkness. Gwen had made a quick study of the geography of the park in the SUV on the way here, but she had taken the precaution of downloading a map of the area, combined with an aerial photo, onto her mobile.

Five minutes later, they were at the lake, and the light from Gwen's torch floated across the shimmering blackness of the lake. It looked as cold and still as slate.

With a hiss of impatience, Jack snapped shut the cover on his wrist-strap.

'Anything?'

'Nothing,' he said. He took a small single-lens night-sight out of a pocket and scanned the lake. 'What exactly am I looking for here?'

'Don't ask me. Ianto said some school kids reported seeing an old woman floating in the lake yesterday afternoon…'

'School kids?'

'It was all over the internet chatrooms, apparently,' Gwen continued.

'Ianto has too much time on his hands.'

'He was searching for specific references – woman, water, local canals, rivers, parks… key words that came up with this.'

'That was yesterday, this is now,' said Jack. 'If she was here then we're too late. This is getting to be a habit.'

A dog barking some way off drew their attention. It wasn't a good bark; there was real aggression in there. The sudden, obsessive noise of an irate dog going in for the attack.

Automatically, Jack was moving towards the noise. 'It's over there,' he said as he picked up speed.

Gwen ran after him, shouting, 'It's only a bloody dog!'

But there was no stopping him now. His greatcoat flapped like a superhero's cape as he circled the lake. The barking grew louder, more frenzied, and Gwen's instincts told her that, whatever was happening, it wasn't right and they needed to stop it. It could be someone under attack, or just a dogfight, but they had to intervene.

They found the dog by the edge of the lake, where the water was covered with a film of green algae and some tangled reeds. It was a pit bull terrier, a fired-up bundle of aggression, its teeth flashing in the moonlight, saliva spraying from its brutish jaws with every bark. It was jumping around the edge of the water, attention focused on something just out of reach.

The dog's owner was with him, a muscular young man, no less brutal than the pit bull, wearing jeans and a hoodie. He was waving a length of chain in the air at the dog and swearing. 'Leave it! Karlo! Leave it I said!' He was bellowing at the dog now, angry as hell but scared too – he'd lost control.

'What's the matter?' Jack wasn't looking at the man or the dog. His attention was directed entirely at the water.

'Stupid bastard saw something in the water,' spat the man. 'Rat, probably. Now he's gone effing mental.'

The dog was barking itself hoarse. Its paws were splashing

at the edge of the water, sending ripples out into the green scum.

'Get back here, you little horror,' the man stepped forward, trying to reattach the lead.

But the dog was having none of it.

'Get it away from the water,' warned Gwen. 'It's not safe.'

'Get lost,' said the man. 'I'm only out walking my dog. Mind your own business.'

'Hey!' said Jack. 'Watch your manners. And get the mutt under control.' He'd raised his voice initially, so that he could be heard over the barking, but at the last moment the dog suddenly fell quiet.

Automatically, they all stopped what they were doing and looked at the pit bull.

It was standing four-square at the edge of the water, flanks heaving as it panted, tongue lolling, drool hanging in thick strings from its jaws.

And then, with a sudden spray of water, something rose out of the lake just in front of the dog with the savage speed of a crocodile.

Gwen didn't even see it properly. She stepped back from the edge of the lake, away from the splashing, her heart hammering in her chest after the initial shock. She could hear Jack shouting something and the dog's owner screaming, but all she could see was the pit bull staggering backwards, minus its head.

She could see it quite clearly, as if the world had slowed to a standstill. The dog's legs were still working, at least for a few moments as its body scrambled away, but the muscles must have been operating on the last vestiges of nervous impulse: at the neck there was only a red stump, blood jetting madly from the severed arteries. Gwen glimpsed a nugget of white bone where the dog's thick vertebrae were still visible, and then the torso gave a final, huge convulsion and lay still.

The water was still boiling. Jack had his gun out, aimed at the lakeside, but there was nothing to see. Algae swilled around his feet, and in the mud Gwen saw the pit bull's head staring out at her from where it had fallen.

The torchlight picked out a wide stream of red in the murky water, and the dog's owner finally realised what had happened. 'God almighty! It's taken his head off!'

'Get back!' Jack ordered.

But the dog's owner was staring in mute, wide-eyed incomprehension at the dead animal at his feet. 'Karlo?'

Jack grabbed the man by the scruff of the neck and dragged him away from the edge of the lake. 'I said get back! Keep away from the water!'

'What the hell was it?'

'Well I don't know!' yelled Jack. 'D'you want to go back and take a closer look?'

The man shook his head, then turned quickly away and vomited.

Gwen ran back to where Jack stood at the lakeside, scanning the swirling green surface for any signs of life. 'Don't get too close,' she warned. 'Did you see what it was?'

'No. Did you?'

'Too fast, just a blur,' she replied. She tried to speak quietly and calmly, to control her racing pulse and natural inclination to panic, fighting down the desire to keep away from the edge of the lake. 'Think the dog had the best view.'

Jack had his gun trained on the water. 'Didn't even see which way it went.'

The dog's owner was walking back towards the lake in a daze. Gwen saw his blinking, disbelieving eyes and recognised the look of a man shocked into a silence that was about to erupt in fury. She could see the spark lurking in his dark eyes as he glared purposefully at Jack.

'Did you do that?' the man said, somewhat unreasonably.

Jack didn't even spare him a glance. 'Easy, fella. We don't know what happened yet.'

The man stepped up, close, squaring his shoulders, legs apart. He jabbed a thick finger at the remains of the pit bull. 'Have you seen that? Have you?'

Jack nodded. 'Kinda hard to miss.'

The man balled a fist, cocking his arm ready to throw the punch, but Jack had seen it coming five seconds before and put the idiot on his backside with one meaty left hook.

'Forget it,' Jack said as the man sprawled in the mud. 'I'm not in the mood.'

The man touched his lip, found it bleeding, and began to get up. It was impossible to tell whether he was going to admit defeat or have another shot but, with a sudden cry of alarm, he fell down again. For a moment, Gwen thought he had simply slipped in the wet mud, but then she realised that he was being dragged into the lake feet first.

Gwen and Jack saw it clearly. Two long, thin arms reached up out of the water, trailing wet, green weeds and grabbed the man around the neck. Bony, twig-like fingers closed around his throat and pulled, hard. Jack didn't know whether to shoot or not – he had the gun trained on the lake, but he was worried he might hit the man if he fired.

The man thrashed madly in the water and then disappeared under the foaming surface with horrifying speed. There was a

140

brief, gurgling skirmish during which a last, desperate shout could be heard bubbling below the surface.

And then nothing but disturbed waves running like rats beneath the blanket of green.

SIXTEEN

Three shots roared into the night air as Jack fired into the churning water. The bullets kicked up a fine mist but struck nothing.

'He was grabbed,' Gwen said, backing away from the lakeside. 'I saw arms – they reached up and pulled him under.'

Jack continued to pace along the edge of the water, gun levelled. 'Call Ianto and Tosh, get them to bring some depth charges from the armoury. We'll blast that thing right out of the water.'

Gwen was already dialling.

When Toshiko answered, her first words were drowned out by a series of harsh coughs. 'Sorry,' she gasped after a moment, 'frog in my throat.'

'We've found the water hag,' said Gwen without preamble. 'It's in the lake in Garron Park. We need depth charges, and fast.'

'Depth charges?' Toshiko's puzzled response was suddenly

overtaken by a tremendous roar from the lake and a shocking blast of water.

'Down!' yelled Jack, turning and hurling himself at Gwen, catching her under the arm with one powerful hand and sweeping her to the floor. She hit the grass winded, but nevertheless had the presence of mind, the fascination, to twist around to see what was happening.

The body of the dog-walker – or what remained of it – landed with a damp thud and a shower of water on the bank. Gwen knelt up for a better look and then regretted it instantly. The man's legs were still intact, but that was about all. The torso had been ripped wide open from groin to chin, clothes and flesh sliced through as if they were nothing more than wet paper. Internal organs protruded from the scarlet wound like spilt shopping from a carrier bag. It looked like the victim of a shark attack, right here on the bank of a small lake in a park in the middle of Cardiff.

The man's head was hanging on by a thin strip of twisted flesh and gristle. Blood was flooding out of the shredded throat and soaking into the earth beneath the man's face, which still bore a rather shocked expression. His eyes were wide but sightless.

With fumbling fingers, Gwen found and drew her pistol. She felt her hands shaking as she disengaged the safety catch and cocked it, already turning in a kneeling position to aim at the lake. Whatever came out next was going to come under heavy fire.

'Gwen?' Toshiko's voice sounded small and far away. 'Gwen? What's going on? What's happened? Gwen, can you hear me?'

'Tosh, I think it's too late for the depth charges,' Gwen

replied eventually. Her mouth had that familiar dryness, the numbing shock of coming face to face with the incredible and the deadly. It was at once terrifying and electrifying, the thought that these next few seconds could be her last on Earth. Her last anywhere.

Flashing blue lights were approaching from the south east, accompanied by the long mournful wail of police sirens.

'Damn,' said Jack quietly.

'Someone's probably reported the dog barking,' said Gwen. 'Asbo time.'

'Look!' Jack shouted, pointing.

Twenty feet away, rising from the lake, was a thin, humanoid shape trailing long wet weeds like the rags of a cloak. Gwen scrambled for her torch, sweeping the beam across the lake, catching the dangling trail of slime as the figure rose higher into the night hair, water gushing from it like a miniature rain cloud.

It floated away into the darkness and Jack immediately sprinted after it, splashing spectacularly through the water.

'Jack!' Gwen called, just as a voice crackled in her ear. She put her hand up to her ear, shouting, 'What?'

'Gwen? It's Owen. I'm on my way to the park. ETA five minutes. Ianto says the cops are heading your way too.'

'Then bloody well step on it, Owen!' Gwen ran around the lakeside after Jack. 'We're chasing a water hag!'

The thing floated no more than ten feet off the ground, trailing weeds and water through the small copse of trees which edged the lake. Jack flew after it, leaping into the air and grabbing hold of the dangling rags. He brought it crashing down into a pile of rotting leaves and mud.

145

'Gotcha!' he roared, only to receive a teeth-rattling blow to the side of his head which sent him reeling. He smashed into a tree, shook his head and then hurled himself on top of the thing again before it could properly regain its feet.

They rolled through the leaves, crashing into a patch of moonlight. Jack sat on top of it and saw a dark, twisted face the colour of mud staring up at him with insane, dirty yellow eyes. A thin mouth broke open to reveal dark, needle-like teeth in pale gums. The creature let out a foul hiss of rage and threw him off with phenomenal strength. Jack whirled, hit the dirt, and then looked up to find the thing pouncing on him. Yellow eyes glared and spit drooled from the dark fangs.

'Naughty Jack!' it screeched at him. She cuffed him across the face, drawing blood. Then she licked his face with a long, cold tongue. 'You taste all wrong!' she said, and spat it back at him. 'You're all messed up, Torchwood boy!'

'OK, now I'm not just intrigued,' said Jack. 'I'm annoyed. Who the hell are you?'

'I'm Sally Blackteeth!'

'Lovely name. Got a boyfriend?'

She leaned down over him and smiled wickedly. 'Professor Len. Did you know him?'

'Bitch,' said Jack.

'Dead meat,' said Sally Blackteeth.

'Him or me?'

'Both.'

She swung at him again, but he was ready for it this time, blocking with his left forearm, letting the wrist-strap take the brunt. She snarled and lashed out again, and this time he used the momentum to roll her off him so that he could swing himself up on top of her. It proved to be a bad move; by some strange anatomical contortion she managed to knee him in the groin. He curled up with a hard grunt of pain but now he could hear that the police sirens were getting much closer. Blue light flickered through the trees.

Sally Blackteeth twisted around, swiping Jack away with the back of one hand as he climbed to his knees. He looked back up just in time to see her disappearing into the glistening darkness and flashing lights.

Jack got back to his feet with a groan just as Gwen came running up. 'It's gone that way,' she panted, grabbing him by the hand and pulling him after her.

'She knew who I was,' Jack said.

They stumbled through the trees and emerged by the lakeside, just as the water hag rose swiftly into the air. Jack pulled his gun and fired, sending two rounds after the fleeing shape.

'Missed her,' said Gwen.

'Shine the light on it!' he yelled, running down into the water, gun arm extended, taking his time now, sighting carefully.

Gwen had automatically counted his shots – three before and a double-tap just now. That left one more bullet in the gun. She waved the torch beam frantically until the light caught something glistening high in the air above.

Jack adjusted his aim, narrowed one eye, squeezed the trigger. The revolver boomed, its final word echoing over the lake before being drowned out by the noise of approaching policemen.

'Armed police! Drop your weapon!' shouted the first man on the scene, dropping to one knee and taking aim at Jack with a steady, two-handed grip on his automatic. 'I said drop your weapon! Now!'

Jack turned around, eyebrow raised.

'This is your final warning,' bellowed the marksman. 'Lower the gun to the ground or I will shoot.'

'Back off,' said Jack. 'It's Torchwood.'

The officer pulled the trigger as the last word left Jack's lips. At this range, the first round was powerful enough to lift him right off his feet, and the second, catching him in the shoulder, spun him right around so that he hit the ground face down in the mud.

The marksman blinked, as if surprised by what he had just done. 'Did he say Torchwood?'

'Hold your fire!' A voice echoed across the park, and Owen Harper strode out of the dark mist. 'Lower your weapons. This entire area is now contained under a Torchwood restriction.'

The police officers were staring in dumb bewilderment at the scene in front of them: a headless dog lying in the mud, an eviscerated human corpse stretched out on the bank, Jack Harkness face down in the water, Gwen standing a little way off looking completely shocked. And Owen striding through them all, right up to the officer in charge until they were nose-to-nose.

'You in charge here?'

'I'm SOCO, yes,' replied the officer stiffly. 'Sergeant Kilshaw.'

'Piss off, then,' said Owen.

'OK, Owen,' Gwen said, walking over. 'I'll handle this now.'

The SOCO turned gratefully towards her. 'Is this true? This is Torchwood business?'

'Yes, I'm afraid so,' Gwen said, mustering a smile from somewhere. She put on her official voice and said, 'I'm afraid we'll have to ask you and your men to leave the area. Thanks for responding, but we'll take over now.'

'Uh... yeah. OK.'

The SOCO looked utterly bewildered, and Gwen softened her tone slightly. 'You could set up a cordon around the park, though. We don't want any innocent nosy parkers getting involved, do we?'

Sergeant Kilshaw nodded, as if only too glad to be given an excuse to withdraw. Then he hesitated, looking down at the gutted corpse dumped on the grass nearby. 'Miss, we have a dead body here. I understand what you're saying, and I know Torchwood has absolute priority, but I don't feel comfortable leaving it like this.'

Gwen held his gaze, steady but not combative. 'I'm sorry, but you said it yourself – absolute priority.'

'I need to find out who he is. We have to inform his family. Can I do that?'

'Not yet. We'll liaise with you and get the details sorted out as soon as.'

Sergeant Kilshaw still wasn't happy, but he knew there was nothing he could do. Yet he paused again, unwilling to leave without claiming some sort of concession. 'What about my man?' He indicated the officer who had shot Jack. Already another member of the firearms team was relieving the marksman of his weapon, and dropping it into a plastic evidence bag for the routine forensic tests that would follow. 'There'll be an enquiry. It's the law.'

'No need,' drawled a voice from the lakeside. Jack was getting slowly to his feet, his face and coat soaked with

149

muddy water and streaked with his own blood. He walked slowly across to the SOCO and smiled. 'No harm done.'

'What?' Kilshaw looked down at the deep red stain spreading across Jack's shirt.

'He missed,' Jack said simply.

The policeman frowned. 'What?'

'Cap'n Jack Harkness,' said Jack warmly. He shook the SOCO's hand and flashed him another bright smile. 'Like I said, no harm done. Get your men together and go, Sergeant. We'll handle things from here.'

'He missed?' repeated Kilshaw, still staring at the blood seeping through Jack's blue shirt.

'Yeah. In fact, I'd reprimand him if I were you. Looks like he needs a bit more practice on the shooting range, wouldn't you say?'

'So where'd it go?' Owen asked a little while later. The three of them were standing by the lake. It was still and deathly quiet. The surface was placid, mirror-smooth under the black night sky.

'Up there, I think.' Jack was looking up at the sky, searching the low clouds tinged with orange from the sodium lights of Cardiff. Spots of rain began to hit his face, making the blood and dirt run.

'You mean she can fly?'

'Crocodile with a jet-pack. She rose up out of the water, and then we lost her in the dark.' Jack looked back down at his revolver, which had its cylinder out so that he could reload. 'Think I winged her, though.'

'It got away again, then.' Owen kicked at the grass in disgust.

'You reckon it's the same thing we saw in the fish farm?'

'Look at the body.' Owen crouched down next to the dog-walker. He used a pencil to indicate the gaping wound, teasing at the torn cloth and flesh. 'This is just like the security guard and Big Guy; practically split him in half.'

Gwen, who had been standing a little apart while she reported back to the Hub, called over. 'I've given Tosh the details. She's going to sort out removal of the body and a suitable story for the cops.'

'What about the press?' asked Jack. 'They'll be all over this place soon.'

'She's on it. She says the press and TV are the easiest to sort out, because brutal murders in local parks are just what they like to hear about and they'll believe anything.' Gwen suppressed a shiver at the thought of Torchwood's cover-up expert going through the routine of disguising their involvement and 'normalising' the incident. It was something Gwen almost took for granted now. Almost. Just like the violent, terrible deaths she had witnessed with incredible regularity since joining Torchwood. She had made a promise to herself, early on and with Jack's encouragement, that she would never become desensitised to it. And yet here she was, staring dispassionately at the eviscerated body at their feet with the same sort of cool, professional detachment that she had seen displayed by the other, experienced members of Torchwood when she first joined the team.

Jack, as ever, seemed to read her thoughts. 'You OK?' he asked softly.

Gwen shrugged and blew out a long, slow breath of mist into the cold night air. 'I dunno, Jack. I don't feel anything. Just a bit sick – but that's the adrenalin climb-down, I think.

You get used to it after a while, I suppose.'

Jack pointed a finger straight down at the corpse. 'Take a good look at him, Gwen. That's a real guy. He was just out walking his dog. He's – what? – around twenty-five, twenty-six. There's a mother somewhere who doesn't even know she's lost him yet. Imagine how she's gonna feel when a cop turns up at her door with the news. Won't matter if her boy was the victim of a gun crime, a backstreet fight, an RTA or an alien psychopath – he's still gone.'

Gwen dragged her eyes off the corpse and looked at Jack. 'Your point being?'

'You've got to care, Gwen. You've told me that often enough – you have to remember to care. He's been murdered by something we just don't understand and we can't find. And it'll do it again unless we do find it, and stop it. That's our job. That's why you have to care.'

She nodded, biting her lip, and turned away.

It was a long walk back to the SUV.

'So, what now?' asked Owen as he and Jack began the trudge up towards the gates after Gwen.

'How'd you get on with the doctor?' Jack asked.

'He's still sick – really sick. He should be quarantined.'

'What's up with him?'

'I don't know. Symptoms indicate some kind of respiratory infection, but it's the worst I've ever seen.'

'Worst as in *The Lancet* worst, or Torchwood worst?'

'Torchwood.' Owen described the strange, subcutaneous movement he had observed at the back of Strong's throat. 'It's nothing that originates on Earth, at any rate. That's why I didn't send him to hospital – it's too risky. Maybe we should

152

bring him back to the Hub.'

'Not if it's contagious,' warned Jack.

'Well I don't know about that.' Owen rubbed his throat and coughed. 'But I think I've caught it.'

SEVENTEEN

Ianto placed the coffee cup carefully next to the Rubik's cube on Toshiko's desk. She was slumped across the workstation, head buried in her folded arms. The various displays on her monitor screens were reflected as blue highlights in her glossy black hair. There were some grapes in a dish buried beneath piles of paperwork and notes, a half-eaten apple and a number of screwed up tissues.

'Tosh?'

She stirred and then, realising that she had fallen asleep at her desk, jerked awake. 'Ianto! Gosh, I must have dropped off…'

'Fresh coffee,' he said smoothly. 'Thought you could do with it.'

She stretched, but not hugely, trying to contain her embarrassment. 'I'm more tired than I thought.'

'Good job Jack didn't catch you sleeping on the job,' Ianto said with a smile. 'How are you feeling?'

'Rough.' The word turned into a series of coughs and

Toshiko reached for her tissues again. 'Oh, I feel so awful. What a time to catch a cold…' She coughed again, more forcefully this time, and tossed the tissue at the waste basket.

It missed and, when Ianto automatically bent down to retrieve the discarded tissue, he could not fail to notice that it contained a small number of red specks. He paused momentarily, wondering if Toshiko knew. She was already back at her keyboard, tapping hurriedly, looking up to see the screens flickering with data.

'There's still nothing here regarding Saskia Harden,' she reported. 'I've double-checked the police criminal records, the national DNA database, Revenue & Customs, Social Services, the lot. I've even tried MI5, Interpol and UNIT. But there's nothing. She just doesn't exist.'

'I thought Owen went to see her GP?'

'The address on their records is false.'

'So who is she?'

Toshiko took off her glasses and chewed the arm thoughtfully. 'Good question. A ghost. A phantom. Or just a figment of someone's imagination?'

'But one who needs a GP.'

'Yes. I wonder why?'

'It's only a guess, but people usually go to the doctor when they're ill.'

Toshiko pointed the arm of her glasses at him and smiled indulgently. 'Hey, you're right. You know, with a brain like that you'll go far, Ianto.'

He smiled. 'Oh, I'm really a genius in disguise. Haven't you worked that out yet?'

'Well, it's a very good disguise.'

'It takes a genius to make a disguise this effective.'

156

Toshiko laughed, and it turned into another cough. She grimaced as the fit passed, rubbing at her neck. 'I've got a sore throat too. Is there anything in the medical stores I could take, Ianto?'

'Basic analgesics is all you're allowed, I'm afraid. There are some alien remedies in the safe, I believe, but they are all strictly out of bounds. Besides which, you are only human. Painkillers designed for Arcateenians, for instance, might not work on you – in fact, quite the reverse: they could be deadly.'

Toshiko shrugged and turned back to her work with a sniff. 'Just my luck.'

'I've checked the TV news,' Ianto told her. 'You may like to know that you're not the only one feeling a bit poorly. There's been a surge of respiratory problems right across South Wales and parts of South West England. They say it's the start of a flu epidemic.'

'It would explain why I feel so lousy.'

'I shouldn't worry too much about it. You're probably just run down, and your experience at Greendown Moss won't have helped.'

Toshiko coughed and groaned again. 'Don't remind me. I don't think I'll ever get the mud out of my hair. But you're probably right. Thanks for the coffee, anyway.'

Ianto deftly removed the cup as soon as she put it down, being very careful not to touch the rim as he did so.

EIGHTEEN

Bob Strong was slowly coming to the conclusion that he was dying. He thought he should call his mother, but he was almost too weak to move.

He was coughing up more blood – thick, dark clots of it mixed with a pungent mucus that made him retch and gag with the effort. He was on his hands and knees, shaking like a frightened dog, spitting out more strings of red slime onto the living room floor, when the doorbell rang.

It was such a stupidly ordinary sound that he almost laughed. Ding dong! Then he was coughing again, and, by the time the convulsions had gone and he was wiping his trembling lips with the remains of a ragged, disintegrating paper towel, he knew there was no way he could get to the door to answer it, let alone care who it was.

The bell sounded again. For a full minute he lay on the cold laminate floor, surrounded by gobbets of blood-streaked phlegm and old tissues, utterly exhausted. When the doorbell sounded for the third and fourth time, each a little more urgently, a part of his semi-conscious brain began to concentrate, analysing the situation, in an almost dreamlike state.

Maybe it was Owen Harper, the man from the Government.

It could be him at the door. With the cure, or some kind of vaccine. Or a team of paramedics in decontamination suits, ready to whisk him into biohazard quarantine. Bob guessed there were procedures, protocols for this sort of thing.

Somehow he dredged up the energy to crawl towards the front door. In the hallway, he had to wait for a minute for another coughing fit to pass, and then, with a mighty effort, pull himself upright using the doorframe as support. Finally, he was on his feet, feeling sick and dizzy, the world spinning around him and an ache in his chest and throat that threatened to stop him breathing. Only then did he think that if it was the authorities, intent on either rescue or internment, they would have probably broken the door down by now and come in for him.

He focused on the front door. There was a shape on the other side of the frosted glass – female.

It took a couple of attempts to open the door because his fingers were half-numb and slippery with perspiration. He couldn't get a good grip on the latch. Eventually he managed to unlock it and the door opened to reveal a young, rather striking blonde in a raincoat. She had strange, haunting green eyes that, even in his current state of mind, he recognised immediately.

'Saskia?'

'Hello, Dr Strong.'

Not 'Good God, you look awful, what's the matter?' Just

'Hello.' It was so utterly normal and unexpected that Bob felt an immediate, fantastic surge of hope and warmth. Maybe things were not quite as bad as he thought, if she didn't reel back in alarm and disgust at the first sight of him. Maybe he felt worse than he looked. But then he remembered who he was dealing with.

'Saskia,' he said roughly, his throat still clogged with snot. Realising this guttural noise could hardly be understood, he swallowed with difficulty and began again. 'Saskia… Y'know, now isn't a good time.'

'Is there anything wrong? You don't look very well, Dr Strong.' Was that a smile on those perfect lips? Surely that was concern in her eyes, not mockery?

Strong went to speak, coughed up another string of mucus, and backed away. Immediately Saskia Harden stepped in after him, reaching out to help keep him upright.

She took him into the living room, surveying the mess without comment. She let him sit down in the armchair. 'Rest there a moment.'

He raised a hand to protest. 'What are you doing here?' He coughed painfully and tried once again to focus on her.

'Do you know what's wrong with you?' Saskia asked him gently.

He shook his head and shivered. 'Dunno. I think it's something to do with what's been on TV. I think I should go to hospital, but…'

'But…?'

'Well, I've already got people working on it,' he told her. 'They've done some blood tests. They're looking in to it.'

'But do you know what it is?'

'Not yet.' He gagged, once, and then spoke in a rush, the

words tumbling from his lips in a hurry because he knew he was going to throw up soon. 'They're saying it's flu but it isn't. I think it's some kind of virus. I mean, virus as in "biohazard". Like a biological weapon – I know it sounds crazy, but I'm convinced. I've seen the reports on the TV… it's spreading across the whole area, and they keep telling everyone it's nothing to worry about, it's just a minor flu epidemic or a bug, but I can tell they're keeping something back. You probably think I'm nuts—' (She shook her head, *not at all*) '—but it feels like there's a wasps' nest in my throat and I can't stop coughing. I want to cough it all up, but it just won't budge. For God's sake, I'm bringing up blood.' He coughed, winced and then said, 'I'm supposed to be a doctor. I can't panic about this. I mustn't.'

He wiped a hand down his face, surprised at the roughness on his chin. He realised that he must look like a complete tramp; Saskia's cool green gaze was still checking him over carefully, perhaps trying to recognise the same man she'd seen in surgery the previous day. 'Look,' he said, summoning a feeble smile from somewhere, 'I did warn you – this isn't a good time for me. Maybe I'm just paranoid or this thing is doing something to my mind, but… Really, what are you doing here?'

She looked at him with a steady, level gaze. 'I've come for my baby, Dr Strong.'

The SUV was speeding back towards Roald Dahl Plass, Owen following in his Honda.

Inside the Torchwood vehicle, the glare of the street lights cast strobing orange shapes across the faces of Gwen and Jack.

'That man,' Gwen said, staring at the road ahead. 'I looked at him properly. And so did you.'

Jack glanced at her but said nothing.

'I saw the way you looked at him.' Gwen turned her head and stared at his profile as he drove. 'The way he'd been killed... cut right open like that. Could you survive something like that, Jack?'

'You know I would.'

'I know you can't die. But a wound like that... how would you? How could you? Surely it wouldn't just... heal?

'It'd take a while, but it would heal. I'd live.'

Gwen shivered. 'I can't imagine that.'

'Try not to think about it,' Jack advised. 'That's what I do.'

She looked back at him. 'But... you must think about it. You must do.'

'Not any more. I don't think about dying. Only living.' He glanced across at her and smiled that wolfish grin. 'Besides, I don't plan on letting anyone rip me open like that. Believe me. That's gotta smart.'

She smiled despite herself. 'Why do you always do that?'

'What?'

'Make me feel daft for even thinking something so bad, even when we're right in the middle of a crisis.'

'Crisis? What crisis?'

'Owen's medical crisis.' Gwen activated the computer console in front of her and went online, searching for a news update. It wasn't hard to find coverage of what the strap line termed 'South Wales Epidemic'.

Owen's voice crackled over the comms. 'How come it's my medical crisis?'

'The TV and internet are full of it,' Gwen reported, tapping at the monitor screen in front of her. 'And they're still calling it a flu epidemic.'

'That's bollocks,' said Owen's voice over the loudspeakers.

'That a medical term?' asked Jack.

'It is when I use it.' The Honda pulled up alongside the SUV as the two cars hurtled along the carriageway. Gwen could see Owen at the wheel. 'Look, it won't be long before someone starts calling it an outbreak,' he continued. 'That's different to an epidemic, by the way. The authorities will already be considering it an emergency, the way things are going.'

'They'll think it's germ warfare or something,' Gwen said. 'Terrorism.'

'They'll check with all the relevant biohazard facilities first – research labs, storage bases, chemical plants, both commercial and government. That won't tell them much. Even if one of them knew there'd been a leak, they wouldn't fess up straight away.'

'What are the chances of it being an accidental leak?' asked Jack.

'Slim, but not impossible.' Owen's voice crackled slightly as the Honda pulled ahead and moved in front.

'What if it's none of those things?' asked Gwen. 'I mean, not an accidental leak from a research lab or even a deliberate attempt at biological terrorism? What if it's something else?'

'Then they'll call us,' said Jack.

'Baby?' said Bob. He suddenly felt a lot worse, if that was possible, as he sensed everything suddenly sliding out of control. 'I don't understand.'

Saskia just smiled. It was the coldest thing Bob had ever seen. 'You will.'

'Saskia, this really isn't the right time…' Bob tried to glare at her, but he couldn't focus properly. He wondered if he was simply hallucinating the whole thing. She looked strangely ephemeral, as if he was seeing her through water.

She pulled off her raincoat, exposing one bare arm for Bob to see.

'You're hurt,' he said, puzzled. The reaction was instinctive. There was a wound – a deep tear in the flesh of her upper arm, crusted with blood. The skin around it was inflamed and swollen. It looked extraordinarily painful, and yet she barely seemed to register it. All this time, and she had not given the slightest indication that it hurt. 'How did you do that?' he wondered. He stared at it, unable to take his eyes off the damage, his professional interest suddenly overwhelming every other thought. 'Is that a gunshot wound?'

This time her lips parted in a tiny snarl. 'Something metal,' she said. Even the word seemed to taste bad for her.

Bob sat up, peering more closely at the wound. It was still bleeding, slightly, but there was something else in there, possibly detritus that would need to be cleaned away.

'You should go to hospital,' he told her. 'The best place for this kind of thing is A&E, honestly.'

As he spoke, he saw something move in the wound. It was dark green, like a fragment of cabbage or broccoli caught in the scab. It quickly withdrew inside the flesh as he looked, almost as if it sensed his observation.

'This is too much,' Bob stammered, looking away. 'I'm seeing things now.'

'Really?'

There was something in her tone – a challenge? A hint of contempt?

Whatever it was, it made Bob look back up at her, into her eyes. And then, in the final moments of his life, Bob suddenly realised what colour Saskia Harden's eyes were.

They were the colour of mucus.

NINETEEN

Jack strode through the giant cog-wheel portal of the Hub and headed straight for the steps on the left leading up to Toshiko's workstation. He was taking the stairs three at a time when he realised that she wasn't at her desk.

'Where's Tosh?' Jack called to Ianto, who was just coming through from the Morgue.

Ianto was holding a dustpan and brush. He used the brush to point. 'Hothouse. Good to see you back.'

'You too, Ianto, you too. Lookin' sharp. I like a man who knows how to keep a place tidy – I ever tell you that?'

'Once or twice.'

Jack doubled back, heading for the spiral steps that led up to the Hothouse. He could see Toshiko now, standing over a complex piece of apparatus in the centre of the room. She was wearing a white lab coat, which stood out among all the plants and bottles. Jack was about to go inside when he realised that the doors were shut, and when he tried to open them he found they were locked.

'Tosh?'

No answer. She was intent on her work and she couldn't hear him through the partition.

Ianto followed Jack up the stairway and cleared his throat apologetically. 'She's sealed herself inside.'

'What? Why?'

Ianto knocked politely on the glass and Toshiko looked up, startled.

Jack felt startled too. Toshiko looked terrible. She was drawn, with dark rings under her eyes and a sheen of sweat over colourless skin. Jack looked back at Ianto. 'What's going on?'

'She's running a temperature and she's as weak as a kitten. Then she started coughing up blood.'

Inside the Hothouse, Toshiko pressed a switch to activate the intercom. 'I've put myself in quarantine, Jack.'

'Quarantine?'

'It's just a precaution. I think I've picked up some kind of infection.' She coughed hard into a handkerchief, holding on to the workbench next to her for support. 'I don't know what it is yet, but I'm trying to isolate it now. I think it could be what's been on the TV news.'

'There must be something we can do. I'll get Owen, he can help.'

'I doubt it,' said Owen, joining them outside the Hothouse with Gwen. He cleared his throat and winced. 'I think I've got it too.'

Jack looked at him. 'Owen, you've got a cold.'

'Man flu,' said Gwen. 'You guys – slightest sign of a sore throat and you hit the deck. Rhys is just the same. Pathetic.'

Jack ignored her and turned back to Toshiko, thumbing the

intercom switch next to the door. 'What you found, Tosh?'

'Well it's not flu, I can tell you that.' Another cough, her face screwing up and a hand going to her throat. 'I've taken blood and saliva samples, I'm testing them now.'

'Owen did all this before, on Saskia Harden's GP. His tests were all clear.'

'I was checking for known diseases,' Owen admitted. He raised a hand to attract Toshiko's attention. 'Are you checking for anything in particular?'

'I'm eliminating any known biological or bacteriological weapons. Sarin, Anthrax, E74. I've even checked for any radioactive isotopes, in case it's plutonium poisoning – the symptoms aren't dissimilar.'

'And?'

'So far it's all clear.'

'Which means?' asked Jack.

Owen said, 'Which means that if it is a bioweapon, it isn't one from Earth.'

'Meeting, downstairs,' Jack told the others, and they moved away towards the stairwell. Jack smiled through the glass at Toshiko. 'Carry on. I'll connect up to you from the Boardroom.'

She nodded wearily and gave him the thumbs up.

Gwen already had BBC News 24 feeding through to the main screen on the Boardroom wall. They were in the middle of a story about the polar ice-caps melting, but the rolling stop-press news at the bottom of the picture referred to the flu epidemic in Wales and southern England. Gwen was reading it out aloud as the others filed in behind her: 'Government scientists have been placed on alert following the outbreak of

169

a previously unknown strain of the flu virus in South Wales and South East England—'

'Government scientists?' said Owen scornfully, sliding into a chair.

'—A spokesperson has denied that the outbreak indicates that bird flu may have made the transition to human beings, although it has yet to be confirmed whether or not this is the deadly H5N1 strain of the virus… Blah blah blah,' Gwen trailed off.

'They're fudging,' agreed Owen. 'They know it's something serious, so they've let slip the bird flu thing. It's a cover for the fact that they haven't a clue.'

'And we do?' said Jack.

'We know it's something to do with Saskia Harden.'

'Do we?'

Owen leaned forward, wincing for a moment as he cleared his throat. 'It's my guess Saskia's the original carrier – Patient Zero. She went to her GP, passed it to him. That's two infected people. Now a contagious pathogen in the middle of a doctor's waiting room, full of people who are already sick or rundown, is the perfect breeding ground. Little or no resistance. Everyone there is infected. They go away, infect other people. And so it goes on.'

'My God, it'll never stop,' whispered Gwen.

'Do you think it's deliberate?' Jack asked. 'Or just an accident?'

'Does it matter?' Owen said. 'Either way we're up the proverbial creek. Remember what happened when the Rift was opened – an entire hospital was brought to its knees trying to deal with fourteenth-century patients with bubonic plague. Something like this could cause the emergency services to go into meltdown.'

'It's deliberate,' Ianto said firmly.

'Why?'

'Think about it. The whole thing boils down to this Saskia woman. Before this week we'd never heard of her – but neither had anyone else, except for the police and her GP. And the records they hold for her are all false. She doesn't really exist.'

'Which is why we have to find her,' said Jack, clicking his fingers.

'And Toshiko?' asked Gwen. 'What do we do about her?'

Jack turned to Owen. 'How do you think she caught it?'

'She must have been exposed to the virus. I don't know how, but it's my guess our dead friend from Greendown Moss is responsible.'

Gwen coughed. 'But if that's the case then we're all infected, aren't we? We were all there in the Autopsy Room.'

They all looked at one another.

Jack opened a link to the Hothouse. 'Tosh? Any news?'

A barrage of strenuous coughing came through the loudspeakers. Eventually, Toshiko's voice, tired and ragged, followed: 'Nothing yet. I think I've managed to isolate a non-human cell, though. It's a slow process. The cells are mutating all the time, almost as if they're trying to disguise themselves as human cells.'

'The likelihood is that we are all infected,' Jack told her.

'I'm the only one showing advanced symptoms so far. I need to stay isolated.' There was a heavy, lonely sigh. Gwen pictured Toshiko lowering herself onto the stool as she talked. 'I'm keeping notes – it starts with a sore throat, then a cough. The cough gets worse… like there's something at the back of your throat but you just can't clear it.'

'Exactly what I've got,' said Owen, and then coughed as if to prove it.

'The cough gets progressively more painful. You begin running a temperature. Eventually you'll find you're coughing up blood.'

Gwen was rubbing nervously at her throat and swallowing repeatedly. 'You know, I'm getting a sore throat too…'

'It's the first sign,' Owen said, looking around the table. 'We've all got it.'

Ianto came into the boardroom, a handkerchief held over his mouth and nose.

'That won't do you any good,' said Owen. 'Holding a hanky over your nose isn't going to protect you against this kind of thing.'

'It's too late for that,' Ianto replied. He showed them the handkerchief – it was full of bright red spots. When they looked back at him, his face was flooded with anxiety. 'What's going to happen to us all?'

'After a while, there will be mucus as well as blood,' croaked Toshiko before dissolving into another fit of coughing. 'From what I can tell, it's at this stage the pathogen becomes properly contagious.'

Gwen felt herself starting to panic. As always, her first instinct was to call Rhys, but she had to shut her eyes tight and ruthlessly close the lid on any thoughts about her immediate future. She wouldn't be any use if she was frozen by fear. Look at Tosh, she told herself. Cool and professional to the end.

To the end… A thought suddenly struck Gwen. 'What about Jack?' she said.

Everyone turned to look at him. 'I never get sick,' he said. 'When you can't die, you don't get bothered much by the common cold.'

'This isn't the common cold,' Gwen said.

'I don't get sick,' Jack repeated. 'Usually.'

There was a long pause. 'Usually?' Owen prompted.

Jack pulled a face and rubbed his neck. 'I've kinda got a sore throat coming on now.'

TWENTY

Owen's mobile rang and he flipped it open. 'Owen Harper.' He listened for a moment and then redialled. 'Voicemail,' he explained, pulling a 'don't know what this is about' face. He waited for the connection and then suddenly had to pull the phone away from his ear as a series of harsh squawks and shouts came out.

It was loud enough to make the others look up. 'What's that?' said Jack. 'Dial-a-fight?'

Ianto had already run a computer check on the signal. 'It's from Bob Strong.'

Owen switched his phone to loudspeaker and replayed the voicemail message. At first, it was difficult to tell what was being said, apart from the fact that it was someone shouting.

'Some kind of argument?' wondered Gwen.

'No, Jack's right, it's a fight,' Owen said.

He replayed the message. They heard a long, inhuman screech which overloaded the phone's mike and then a series of frightened yells – the sound of a man in fear of his life. 'That's

Bob Strong,' Owen said. The sounds grew incomprehensible – except for Strong's one, final word, which echoed loudly around the boardroom:

'Saskia!'

Then there was a heavy thud, followed by a long, wet ripping sound. Silence. Coarse breathing approaching the phone. A click and then nothing.

Owen shot out of his seat and was already halfway to the stairs by the time the others ran out after him. 'We'll all go,' Jack called after him. 'Get the SUV.' He turned to Ianto. 'Stay here, keep an eye on Tosh, let me know the moment anything happens. Got it?'

'Anything?'

'Yeah – like if she finds a cure, I'm the first to know.'

'Actually, she'd be the first to know, technically. And I'd be second. That would make you third, at best.'

'OK, if she finds a cure, I want to be the third to know. Happy?'

'Anything else?'

'Get onto the traffic police, clear a route to Bob Strong's house.'

Jack drove, flooring the accelerator, sending the SUV tearing along the night-time roads towards Trynsel. Owen sat in the passenger seat, coughing continuously into a handkerchief. 'We won't get there in time,' he gasped. 'He's dead. Saskia Harden killed him, you all heard it.'

Gwen sat in the back, checking the monitors linked to the Hub, massaging her burning throat. She immersed herself in the work, trying her best not to think about what was happening to her – to all of them. 'We don't know what's happened yet, Owen. That's just supposition. All we know is that he said her name. Doesn't mean a thing.'

Owen said nothing. He felt too ill to argue.

Ianto had done his usual superb job with the police. The roads were clear, and Jack kept the SUV on or around 80 mph where he had to, pushing it up to the 100 mark on the longer roads.

The SUV skidded to a halt outside Strong's house. The front door was open.

Bob Strong lay in the middle of the living-room floor, face up. He looked pale but peaceful. There was dried blood on his lips. Owen stooped over the body, a cursory examination confirming the worst. 'He's gone,' he said, after failing to find a pulse.

'This place stinks,' said Gwen, covering her mouth as she gagged and coughed. 'Urgh. Rotten cabbage or something.'

Jack checked the kitchen. 'Nothing in here,' he said.

'Wait,' Gwen called suddenly. She pointed at the corpse. 'I thought I saw a pulse.'

'You can't have,' argued Owen. 'He's dead. D-E-D dead.'

She looked at him, and he knew immediately what she was thinking.

After only a moment's hesitation, Owen knelt back down by Strong's head and felt again for a pulse. After trying several times to find the carotid artery, he shook his head. 'Nothing. Nada. Zero. Zilch.' He withdrew his hand and, as he did so, froze. He was still looking at Strong's neck. 'Wait a sec…'

'It moved, didn't it?' said Gwen. She was standing still, staring at the corpse, wanting to be wrong.

'What's going on?' asked Jack.

Owen pointed. A moment later, the flesh in Strong's

neck rippled as something moved beneath the surface. The movement caused the man's head to sway grotesquely from side to side, like some kind of puppet. Then, suddenly, the corpse gave a huge spasm and started to cough and splutter like a drowning man.

'Here we go again,' said Jack.

Owen stepped back, giving the corpse room to move. Jack had his gun out, covering the body as it jerked and convulsed. 'Y'know, I kind of prefer it when the dead stay dead.'

'Pot. Kettle. Black,' Owen said.

'Yeah,' agreed Jack with a shrug. 'The difference is, I do it with style.'

Strong was climbing unsteadily to his knees. His eyes were still closed, his face grey and slack. After a moment his mouth opened and he said, 'Owen Harper? Is that you...?'

'Yeah.' Owen swallowed. 'I'd say welcome back, but...'

'It's Saskia,' gasped Strong, straining to get the words out as his throat constricted and he doubled up in agony. 'Saskia Harden...'

'Where is she?' demanded Jack.

Strong turned, twisting violently from side to side, unable to speak or even draw breath. Then he gave an almighty cough; a loud, barking hack that sounded like the beginning of projectile vomiting but produced nothing. For a moment he continued to dry retch on his knees, head back, mouth open. Then, without warning, a sudden gush of blood ran down his chin, followed by a long, choking cry that only stopped when something rose up in his throat and filled his mouth like a plug. His jaws widened, cracked, the lips stretched back in a taut rictus around his teeth as something began to force its way out of his mouth.

It emerged with sickening speed, like a newborn baby slipping free of the womb in a stream of fluid. Then Bob's throat burst open with a spray of blood across the floor and the homunculus climbed free. The glistening green figure landed in a pool of gore, slipping and sliding but quickly righting itself as Bob's corpse finally toppled backwards. The body simply fell back to the floor like a dropped glove.

Owen, suddenly galvanised into action after watching the process with horrified fascination, drew his gun.

'Don't shoot!' yelled Jack, holding a hand out to warn him off. 'Don't shoot. I want it alive.'

But the homunculus had other ideas. With a hiss it scampered across the floor, leaving a trail of red slime as it disappeared through the door.

'Damn!' Even if Jack wanted it alive, he didn't want it to escape, so he followed the thing with his gun, firing as it went. The shots tore up long splinters of wood laminate but not one hit the creature.

The homunculus moved preternaturally fast; by the time Gwen had followed it outside and reached the pavement, it had vanished into the night. She swore and turned back.

Owen was examining Bob Strong's remains where he had fallen on the living-room floor. There was blood everywhere, and the lower half of his face had been completely torn away, exposing the raw meat of his throat.

Jack stood over the body, fist to his mouth as he began to cough. 'Same as the Greendown man?'

Owen nodded, indicating the gaping fissure in the man's neck. 'It was growing in there all the time.'

Jack swallowed hard. 'You said you saw something moving

179

in his throat when you examined him earlier today. The homunculus?'

They all stared at Bob Strong's shattered jaws and ravaged neck. Then they all looked at each other.

Gwen was pale and sweating. She massaged her throat and gagged. 'It starts with a sore throat,' she whispered. 'Oh my God, no…'

'We've all got it,' Owen realised, his own hand on his neck. 'One of those things – growing inside us…'

'Not just us,' Jack said. 'All the people from Strong's surgery. All the people they may have infected. All of them carrying one of those things. Incubating it. Waiting for it to…'

'To what?' Gwen asked loudly, fear making her angry. 'To climb out?'

'To be born.'

Gwen had never felt so sick. She staggered over to the window, leaning on the sill. Dimly, she could hear Jack contacting Ianto, asking him for a situation report between coughs. On the other side of the room, Owen leaned against a wall, pale and shaking as he hacked into his hand. It came away speckled with blood.

Then, bizarrely, the telephone rang. It was a cordless handset on the coffee table. They all stared at it as it rang again. Then Jack picked it up. 'Hello?'

'Hello? Is that you, Bob?'

Jack cleared his throat. 'No. I'm afraid Bob's not available. Who's calling?'

'Well – it's his mother,' said the voice cautiously. 'I was just calling to see how he is…'

Jack looked down at the dead man on the floor.

'Mrs Strong?'

'Yes?'

'I'm Captain Jack Harkness. We need to talk, but I'm afraid I have some very bad news for you.'

Ten minutes later, Gwen was staring out of the window. Jack had finished speaking to Mrs Strong. Gwen had hardly dared to listen; she had been the bearer of bad news to unsuspecting relatives too many times already. It was never a good experience.

She stood in a kind of trance, hearing Jack's words but not listening to them. People were walking past, going about their everyday business, oblivious to the abject horror being played out in this ordinary suburban living room. Cars swished by, drivers intent on the road.

On the pavement opposite, a severe-looking blonde woman stared back at Gwen. She was wearing a raincoat and cradling a baby in her arms. At least, Gwen thought it was a baby at first, but actually it was more like a toddler, a child perhaps only three or four years old. The child turned to look at Gwen as well, and an abrupt coldness filled her like ice water.

It was the homunculus. The face, a parody of a human's features, was still covered in blood and mucus. The sharp little eyes, yellow and calculating, watched Gwen from either side of a sharp, blade-like nose and a vicious little slit of a mouth. The slit opened in a smile, showing black, needle-like teeth.

'Owen,' Gwen croaked.

He joined her at the window and saw the woman carrying the homunculus.

'It's her,' he said. 'Saskia Harden. And that's her new baby.'

181

TWENTY-ONE

They ran outside, but the woman and the homunculus had already gone.

'That can't have been it,' Owen said, shaking his head. 'It was way too big. Two or three times the size of what we saw. That wasn't what Bob Strong just coughed up.'

'I tell you it was,' Gwen insisted. 'I know it was. It's grown, even in that short a time. I could tell by the way it looked at me. By the way she looked at me.'

'Saskia Harden,' Owen spat the name out like a lump of phlegm. 'I've never even met her and I'm getting to really hate that bitch.' He coughed heavily, turning his head politely away from Gwen as he did so. When he looked back at her his face was grey and his eyes were red and watering. 'Come on,' he said huskily. 'Let's move. We need to get this place sealed off first, though.'

Owen collected some hazard tape from the SUV and stretched it across the front door of Strong's house as a makeshift barrier, while Gwen called in a police SOC team to cordon the area off. She wasn't in any mood for the questions they asked and cut them off abruptly by pulling rank. The power Torchwood gave her was usually a secret thrill, but right now it just made her feel nauseous.

What made it worse was when the young policewoman on the other end of the phone line started to cough, apologising immediately afterwards. 'Sorry,' she said. 'Must be that flu thing. I think we're all coming down with it… They say it's nothing to be alarmed about, but they don't tell us anything really. I've seen the TV pictures, just like everyone. Of course we're alarmed, what do they expect?'

'Yeah,' said Gwen dully, as the WPC started coughing again. 'Thanks, anyway.'

Jack drove them back to the Hub. He had been very quiet following his conversation with Mrs Strong, listening silently to a report from Ianto.

'Tosh has made some progress. She's isolated the alien cells from her own body and matched them with those she found in the Greendown Moss corpse.'

'Quelle surprise,' muttered Owen. His head was resting against the passenger window and he had his eyes shut. His face was grey and shiny with sweat, reflecting the flashing blue lights which ran up the sides of the SUV windscreen.

Toshiko was struggling to focus. Not the ideal thing for carrying out delicate experiments in a controlled environment. Not that any of this was very controlled. Her vision kept blurring and her hands were shaking as she adjusted the controls on the microscope. It took every ounce of her self-control to keep her mind on the job, to ignore the sound of her heart thudding in her chest, the pounding of the blood in her head. She knew she was close to finding what she was looking for, she just had to keep concentrating.

She had to keep stopping to cough as well. She had hoped that the warm, humid atmosphere of the Hothouse would help – in theory, it should have kept the respiratory passages clear and open. It was a common and simple remedy for croup, after all. But now it felt like there was something at the back of her throat, swelling all the time, threatening to choke her, and she just couldn't dislodge it. On a number of occasions she found herself on her knees, or lying on the floor, utterly spent with the effort of coughing.

Then, when she finally found the strength to pick herself up and carry on, she would grab a tissue, wipe her chin, lean against the workbench and tell herself not to give up. Just carry on. Don't think of anything else but the work.

There was a knock on the glass door behind her. She turned around and saw Ianto; a large pot plant partially obscured his face, but she could see that he wasn't well either. His face was pale and drawn and there was a thin rime of blood on his lips.

'Why don't you come out?' he said through the intercom. His voice sound hoarse. 'You need a break.'

'No. Got to keep working.'

'There's no point remaining in quarantine,' Ianto pointed out. 'We're all infected.'

'It's OK.' She managed a faint smile. 'I work better alone like this. The isolation helps concentrate the mind.'

'The others are on their way back to base,' Ianto told her. 'They'll be here soon.'

'That's good. Any news from the outside world?'

'Nothing good. The flu story isn't being accepted. Perhaps

people aren't as gullible as the Government hoped. They've changed their minds now and they're saying it's an isolated outbreak of a tropical disease. Nothing to worry about, no serious risk to the public, no need to panic, but they're sending in specialist army medical teams to various locations across South Wales and England to help relieve the pressure on local doctors and hospitals.'

'They've no idea what they're dealing with,' said Toshiko.

'Do we?'

In the SUV, Ianto's voice came through, husky and pained: 'Jack, I have a call for you. It's the PM.'

'Now?' Jack snapped. 'All right, put him through.' Jack took a hand off the wheel and tried to clear his throat, which turned into a full-on coughing session before he could resume speaking. 'Hello, Prime Minister,' he croaked. He listened for a moment and then said, 'No, sir, the situation is not under control. Yes, I know it's fast becoming an emergency. And yes, Torchwood is doing everything it can to resolve the situation.'

He listened for a minute longer, his face grim in the light of the dashboard. 'With respect, sir, we don't operate on those lines. If you want to flood the area with troops in NBC gear then that's your call. It won't affect what we're doing. But no, I don't think it's a good idea. For one thing it won't do a damn bit of good and it'll probably start a panic… No, I should think the Home Secretary is probably safe. There is no need for him and the rest of the Cabinet to go into the secure facility… Oh, you already are. OK, well you sit tight, sir, and don't worry. And tell the Home Secretary it's probably just a cold. We'll handle things from here.'

Jack broke the connection and bared his teeth in feral anger. 'Dumbass. He thinks we're responsible.'

'Us?' queried Gwen incredulously.

'The disease is concentrated around the Cardiff area and South Wales. Of course, it's started to affect some areas in England, so now Westminster's worried. The finger is being pointed at Torchwood.'

'It must be something to do with the Rift,' Owen pointed out. 'It's connected somehow.'

They had to cross through the Trynsel area, and Owen realised that they were passing near the medical centre. But the first thing they saw was a lot of police cars, blue lights flashing, then a fleet of ambulances. Paramedics and cops were walking around, heads down.

'What's going on?' wondered Gwen.

'We're near the medical centre where Bob Strong worked.'

'Where he first met Saskia Harden,' Jack added.

A policeman in a florescent hi-vis vest waved them down. Jack pulled up and opened the driver's window. As the SUV slowed, the cop saw the word TORCHWOOD stencilled on the wing and immediately stiffened, practically coming to attention. 'Sorry, sir, didn't realise it was you,' he said. He covered his mouth and coughed painfully. 'We're trying to cordon off the area,' he continued. 'So we're redirecting traffic. Just waiting for the diversion signs, see.'

Beyond the last police car, they could see a pair of army medical trucks, large red crosses on the khaki sides. Soldiers were pulling on white one-piece overalls and transparent plastic helmets.

The policeman noted Jack's look and said, 'It's just a precaution – leastways, that's what they're telling us. I don't

187

believe anything they say any more. Do you lot know what's happening, sir? Only I'm from around here, and I know a lot of people who've got the blood cough, see.' He reached into his pocket and produced a handkerchief smeared with red. 'Myself included. My sergeant says I can't go off duty, though. All leave's been cancelled. Half the boys are sick and my missus, well, she's very worried. We've got two kids, you know…'

Jack looked up at him. The cop was no more than twenty-three, maybe twenty-four. Behind him the troops were getting their Nuclear-Biological-Chemical suits sorted. 'Don't worry,' Jack told him. He smiled. 'We're on it.'

The policeman waved the SUV through, and Jack accelerated towards the city centre, calling in to Ianto as he went.

'Tell Toshiko we need results and fast. This thing's officially out of control.'

'That might be difficult,' replied Ianto. His voice sounded strained, but he was doing his best to stay calm and professional.

'What gives?' Jack demanded, his knuckles whitening on the steering wheel.

'I've just been to check on Tosh. She's unconscious.'

They took the quickest route to the Hub – pulling up with a screech of brakes by the Millennium Centre and sprinting to the water tower. There was just enough room for the three of them on the paving slab that doubled as a lift platform. No one else could see them – or at least no one else could notice them – when they stood on that particular paving stone right in front of the tower. Jack operated the lift using the remote control built into his wrist-strap and the paving stone began to descend, sliding beneath the ground.

Gwen started coughing, twisting around, away from the others, as the pain stabbed through her. As the mirrored surface of the fountain start to rise above her, Gwen spotted the reflection of a woman staring back at her: thin, blonde, raincoat. Saskia Harden. Reacting instinctively, Gwen leapt off the plinth as it dropped below ground level, scrambling onto the pavement. Several passers-by looked around in shock as she seemed to appear from nowhere.

Jack's voice was already crackling in Gwen's ear: 'Gwen, what's up?'

'I've just seen Saskia Harden,' she gasped, regaining her feet, turning in a slow circle as she scanned the area. 'Oh my God, Jack, she was looking right at us. She could see us. The perception filter didn't work.'

The paving stone sank into the Hub. Jack had one hand to his ear as he talked. 'How could she get here so fast?'

'I've no idea.'

'Maybe she knows where the Rift is,' suggested Owen.

'Still doesn't explain how she beat us here,' they heard Gwen say.

Jack gritted his teeth, annoyed. 'Either way, she knows we're here. What's she want?'

'I can't see her now,' Gwen said. 'I've lost her. She must be here somewhere...' Her voice wavered as she talked and moved.

'Keep looking. We'll deal with things down here. Stay in touch and don't take any risks.' Jack jumped down from the paving-stone platform before it had come to a halt and ran across the Hub and up to the Hothouse. Ianto was already there, inside, trying to resuscitate Toshiko. He was bent over her, head down, mouth to mouth. Owen hurried through, sliding past Ianto, quickly taking over.

'Tosh? It's me, Owen.' He pulled back an eyelid, felt for her pulse. Listened to her chest. 'You did all right,' he told Ianto hurriedly. 'She's still breathing. Good job.'

'You broke the seal,' Jack said to Ianto as he walked slowly out of the Hothouse.

Ianto looked shaken. 'What else could I do? Tosh was just lying on the floor. She wasn't moving. I thought she was…'

'It doesn't matter,' Jack told him softly.

Ianto's lips tightened but he didn't reply. His gaze was fixed on Owen as he worked, listening as he muttered non-stop to the inert figure. 'Tosh? Toshiko? Can you hear me? Come on, Tosh… Give me a sign…'

Ianto swallowed and coughed. 'I came down to see how she was doing. I knew she was weak, but… I found her there on the floor. She wasn't moving.' He took a deep, shuddering breath and dragged a hand down his face. 'I didn't know what to do… We were all relying on her.'

Jack touched Ianto's arm. 'Hey. You did the right thing.'

Ianto looked at Jack, took in his pale, sweating features – so unlike the vibrant, full-of-life man he knew so well. 'We're all dying, aren't we?'

'We're not dead yet,' Jack told him. 'And we've got a job to do – all of us. Gwen saw Saskia Harden just before we came down. She's searching the area now, but she needs help. Go check the CCTV. Work with Gwen. Find Saskia for me.'

Ianto nodded and moved away.

Jack stepped into the Hothouse and knelt down by Owen.

Toshiko was lying in the recovery position, flecks of dried blood on her pale lips. She looked uncomfortably like Bob Strong had when they'd found him on his living room floor. 'How is she?'

'She's spark out. I can't get a response although the pulse is steady. She's breathing OK.'

'You know what I mean,' Jack said.

For a few moments, Owen was taken over by another coughing fit, bringing up blood which he spat to one side. Eventually he said, 'If you mean, is Tosh about to throw up one of those things then I don't know. Maybe. Probably.'

Jack surveyed the detritus around the Hothouse – discarded test tubes, specimen jars, slides, paperwork, tissues. The tangled remains of a fallen rubber plant. Some blood, coughed up and then smudged across the floor. This didn't look like somewhere Toshiko had been working. She was usually neat and methodical, the epitome of a scientist. Everything in its place and a place for everything. But now even her white lab coat was covered in red stains.

'It'll kill her,' Jack said.

TWENTY-TWO

Gwen stopped to lean against the rail as another coughing fit came. She was shaking and her head was pounding. She hacked and coughed and then spat the result out into the bay. After a few moments, the cold wind blowing in across the water started to refresh her, flicking her hair back from her face, drying out the sweat.

She took a deep breath of the freezing air and stood up straight. This was no time to be ill. She had a duty to perform. With an effort she turned around, leant against the rail with her back to the bay and turned her full attention on Roald Dahl Plass. She could see the water tower and the bronze armadillo shape of the Millennium Centre. There were plenty of people around, but she couldn't see any tall blonde in a raincoat. There were a hundred places she could have gone, heading away from the Centre, into the cafés and restaurants which surrounded the area, or further into the city. But somehow she didn't think Saskia had gone. All her instincts told her that the woman was here somewhere. Why else would she come and stand there, watching them, waiting for them? Her business was here, with Torchwood, with the Rift itself.

'Gwen?' Ianto's voice. He sounded rough. She wondered if she sounded as bad to him, and thought that she probably did. 'I'm checking all the CCTV cameras in the area. No sign of Saskia Harden as yet.'

'OK, good,' Gwen responded. 'Keep checking. She's here somewhere, I'm sure of it.' She started back towards the Plass, looking everywhere but still talking. 'How's Tosh?'

'Not good.'

'OK.' Gwen swallowed with difficulty and pushed on. She watched a patrol car coming from the direction of Lloyd George Avenue, blues and twos going like mad. She wondered how long it would be before there were ambulances here and army trucks and soldiers in NBC kit.

Jack and Owen lifted Toshiko onto the autopsy table. Neither of the men would look at each other; neither wanted to be the one to acknowledge what this felt like. All the time, Owen was muttering under his breath, 'She's gonna be fine, she's gonna be fine,' as he busied himself around the room, gathering equipment, wheeling monitors over to the table, plugging in cables.

Jack slumped against the stairs, hands cupped over his mouth as he coughed again. He knew from the taste that there was blood, a lot of it, and something else, too. A thick, foul slime he was bringing up from Hell itself. He spat it out into a cardboard dish and groaned.

'This going to work?' he asked eventually.

'How do I know?' Owen retorted. He was powering up a piece of machinery by the side of the autopsy table. He still wouldn't look directly at Toshiko's still body. 'We've got to be sure, though, haven't we? We can't do anything until we're sure.'

'OK,' Jack agreed, pushing himself upright. 'Let's do it.'

'We haven't got time for a proper X-ray,' Owen said as he operated the controls on the monitor. 'This should do just as well, though. Ultrasound scanner – just like they use on pregnant women.'

They exchanged a look. Jack scowled, and Owen swallowed, turning his attention back to the equipment. 'OK, we're set.'

He took hold of the scanner, making sure there was enough flex on it to use properly. Then he nodded at Toshiko. 'Open her top.'

Jack pushed the lapels of her lab coat aside and then pulled the neck of her top down away from her throat. Owen spread some clear gel around the skin of her neck and chest with his free hand and then placed the scanner against the flesh.

The screen showed a fuzzy mixture of lines and shapes like a particularly bad TV reception. It looked like nothing to Jack, who said so.

'Wait while I get my bearings,' Owen told him, twisting around so that he could check the view on the screen while he moved the scanner. 'Ribs. Sternum. Thorax.' He pulled a face. 'Looks OK to me.'

'Would one of those things show up on that?'

'No reason why it shouldn't, even if it's very small. Which, judging by the thing that came out of Bob Strong's throat, it won't be.' Owen moved the scanner into a different position, monitoring the result carefully as the grey smudges on the screen shifted and coalesced. 'I can't see anything,' he said at last.

'Can't see anything as in you can't tell, or can't see anything as in she's all clear?'

He shrugged. 'As far as I can tell, she's all clear.'

Jack frowned. 'How can that be? She's had all the symptoms. Hell, we all have…'

Owen switched the scanner off and put it down on the tray by the monitor. 'I don't understand it.'

'That's because you're a man,' said Toshiko weakly.

Gwen had circled right around the Plass and was now standing directly in front of the water tower.

'Any sign?' she asked, still scanning. The wind from the bay made her eyes water. She had to keep blinking to make sure her vision wasn't compromised.

'Nothing,' Ianto's voice sounded in her ear. 'I've combed the area three times and run a face-recognition program we stole from the FBI. Anyone who's even looked towards one of the cameras has been checked by computer, but no hits for Saskia Harden.'

'She's here somewhere, I know she is,' Gwen murmured.

'Very perceptive of you,' said a voice behind her.

Gwen whirled around – but there was no one there. She stared at her reflection in the tower, rippling under the constant flow of water which slid down the mirrored surface.

A soft laugh tinkled like glass in the water.

Just for a second, Gwen thought she saw a face in the water: thin, sharp, silvery like a slug trail. She caught her breath, surprised, and then the face was gone, dissolving into the flow of the water like a mirage.

Gwen felt the hairs on her arms and neck stirring. There

was something here, something unnatural. Something she should notice.

And then, with a slow, cold dread, she realised what she had missed. It was so obvious she wanted to shout, to kick, to scream out loud. But all she could do was cough, and point. 'I can see you,' she gasped, pointing at the fountain. 'I know you're there.'

And the simple realisation of it allowed her to see, to perceive, what no one else around her could. Standing on the paving slab right in front of the fountain, right in front of her, was Saskia Harden.

She seemed to be tall, although she was only Gwen's height. She still gave the impression that she was looking down, though, with eyes that were as cold as the morning frost on a lawn. Her skin almost white, her lips wide and slightly parted. There was only a glimpse of darkness between them. She wasn't beautiful, or even pretty, but she was striking. In a room full of gorgeous women, it would be Saskia Harden that all the men turned to look at.

'Took you long enough,' she said to Gwen. Her voice was as cool as mist.

'Standing on that paving stone,' Gwen muttered. 'You've got quite a nerve.'

'Works, though, doesn't it? Not even you could see me – not even when you were looking right at me. What is it? Perception filter? Chameleon field?'

Gwen stood very still. She tried to concentrate, to gather herself, to ask the right questions and say the right things, but her head felt muzzy and her chest and throat hurt like hell. 'What are you doing here?' she asked eventually.

'Taking over,' Saskia replied.

'I mean here, now, at Torchwood.'

'Checking out the competition, of course,' she replied, casting a quick, cold glance up and down Gwen. 'Can't say I'm worried.'

'We're not competition. We don't want to take over the world.'

She shrugged. 'Maybe not – but you're the only ones who will try to stop me.'

'Sooner than you think,' Gwen said, reaching behind her waist for her gun.

'No.' Saskia raised one long finger, curling it like a talon. Gwen felt herself stop, fingers barely touching the metal of the automatic stuffed into the back pocket of her jeans. She knew she should draw, knew she should aim and fire in one smooth motion, but somehow she couldn't move. She had to see what the woman was going to say.

'No,' Saskia repeated. 'Not advisable, dear. I can move a lot faster than you can. I'd bite your head off before you'd even got a hand on your weapon. And we wouldn't want that, now, would we? I'm still picking dog hairs out of my teeth after all.'

She smiled – a wide, wide smile that told Gwen this was no human being. This was a creature capable of biting the head off a pit bull terrier. The lips had parted and for a second she saw the teeth inside – rows of sharp, uneven little spikes like clusters of dark knitting needles.

'What are you? Where are you from?'

'It hardly matters. It was such a long time ago.' Without seeming to care that she was taking her eyes off Gwen, Saskia tilted her head slightly so that she could look briefly up to heaven. 'My world disappeared – vanished without trace.

I came here because I had to. There was nowhere else for me to go. Sad, but here I am. And here you are – but not for long…'

Gwen coughed, crunching up as the pain ripped through her chest, covering her mouth automatically. She spat the blood onto the ground between her feet, breathing hard.

'Oh dear,' said Saskia. 'Not feeling very well?'

TWENTY-THREE

Toshiko's eyes were blinking open. They looked raw, but she was fully conscious. Jack and Owen simply looked at her, open-mouthed. She raised a hand weakly, and Owen instantly reached out and grabbed it, holding it tight in both hands. Toshiko opened her mouth and said, 'I… feel… all right.'

'Well you look bloody awful,' said Owen.

'I mean… I'm alive.' Toshiko took a breath and then coughed, painfully, and Jack, moving suddenly, helped her into a sitting position.

'Boy are we glad to see you!' Jack gasped.

Owen was frowning. 'Here, what did you mean, "because I'm a man"?'

'Wrong sex,' Toshiko smiled weakly, pulling herself into a sitting position with some help from Jack. 'I worked it out in the lab, but I… I just couldn't go on… I was so tired.' Her voice disappeared into a faint croak. 'Mouth's so dry.'

Owen gave her a glass of water from the sink. 'Drink this.'

She gulped at the water greedily, wiping her mouth on her sleeve, trying not to gag or cough again. Then she put an air of professionalism on like a coat and said, 'Check yourselves using the ultrasound.'

Owen switched the scanner on, and, not bothering with any gel, pulled open the neck of his shirt and placed it on the flesh of his throat. He coughed, and the image on the monitor spasmed in time.

Jack peered closely. 'Still looks like a blur to me.'

Toshiko pointed. 'No, look. There.' She traced a fuzzy shape on the screen with her finger. 'See that lighter patch? Hold the scanner still. Stop coughing. There! That's it...'

The shape on the monitor suddenly came into a kind of focus. A grey, foetal shape. Like a tiny doll that had been pushed into a ball. As they watched, it moved slightly, changing position like someone asleep. Owen coughed again.

'Homunculus,' said Jack quietly.

Abruptly Owen yanked the scanner away from his throat and began to gag, turning to throw up into the sink. He coughed and spat out blood and a heavy amount of slime. 'I can feel it moving,' he gasped. 'Inside.'

Jack grabbed the scanner and put it against his own neck. After a moment's examination, the same picture appeared out of the grainy blur on the screen. 'Me too,' he said.

'Because you're male,' Toshiko told them. She sank back onto the autopsy table. 'I managed to isolate the alien cells. They're formed by minute spores which lodge in the mucus membrane of the throat. They're a kind of bacteria, but one that it is infinitely more complex and adaptable than any kind of bacteria on Earth...'

'Take it easy, Tosh,' warned Jack. He put an arm around her and helped her back into a sitting position.

She leaned heavily on him but shook her head. 'There's no time for that. I have to tell you all this. The alien bacterium infects the throat, causing the swelling and sores which it feeds on as it grows. But the spores require a certain chemical to begin the transmutation process – testosterone, and lots of it.'

'So what are you saying?' Jack asked. 'It only affects guys?'

'Yes, in a word. Both men and women get the symptoms – but only the male of the species goes on to fertilise the spores and grow a new homunculus.'

Owen boggled. 'You mean I'm pregnant?'

'Well…'

'But I'm always so careful.'

Toshiko smiled despite herself. 'It's not technically a pregnancy, any more than it would be a pregnancy if a tropical fly laid its eggs under your skin and allowed you to incubate them until they hatched. The homunculus is more of a parasite in that respect. It uses you, feeds off you, and then, when it reaches maturity, it emerges.'

'Killing the host,' Owen realised.

'Wait a sec,' Jack interrupted. 'Maturity?'

Toshiko nodded weakly. She was still far from well, but she was pushing herself to make the report, her voice hoarse and cracking as she spoke. 'The alien mucus cells multiply at an incredible rate… completely unlike anything found on Earth… The creature that grows is alien, but it takes on many of the aspects of its host's DNA – not incorporating it but copying it. Using it like blueprints or plans, if you like. So at a very basic level it has two arms, two legs and a head simply because its host does. But what finally emerges is not an infant. It's mature, but just not fully grown. A true homunculus.'

'But it carries on growing,' Jack said. 'We saw it happen – that thing Bob Strong threw up, it was really small, but when Gwen saw it outside it had grown two or three times as big in minutes.'

'That's about it, yes.'

'So there's another fully grown one of these things out there,' Owen said.

Jack was already running up the steps out of the Autopsy Room. 'Ianto! What's going on with Gwen?'

Ianto turned to look at Jack as he bounded up to Toshiko's workstation. 'It's not good. Gwen's found Saskia Harden…'

'What?' Jack bent over the desk and peered at the monitor screen, which showed a view outside the Hub – directly above them, in fact, right in front of the water tower. Gwen was standing talking to a blonde woman in a raincoat.

'She's… unusual,' Ianto conceded.

Jack raised an eyebrow. 'I like unusual.'

'Well, I know that, but…'

'She is kind of cute, though, isn't she?' Jack grinned wolfishly at him. 'In a bite-your-head-off way.' Then the smile died in an instant, his jaw hardening. 'And I mean that literally. She's a stone-cold killer, Ianto, a vicious predator from another world. She's made from bile and snot and blood and stagnant water, but she can make it look any way she wants.'

'Like sugar and spice and all things nice,' Ianto murmured, fascinated.

'Yeah.' Jack was suddenly overtaken by severe chest cramps and a harsh, tearing cough. He collapsed onto the desk, slid to one side, doubled up in pain. The blood bubbled on his lips. 'Ah, hell...' he groaned, spitting it away. 'It's getting bad...'

Ianto was coughing too. 'I... I can feel it in my throat... moving, squirming around... I want to cough it up but I can't.'

'Don't worry, you will,' Owen said as he joined them. 'When it's good and ready it'll come all right.'

Toshiko arrived, shooing Ianto out of her seat and taking her place at the keyboards. She scanned the screens with an expert eye.

'What are you doing here?' asked Jack. He was leaning against the rail like a boxer on the ropes. 'Tosh, you have to rest...'

'She can't rest,' Owen said. He was sinking to his knees by the workstation. 'We need her.'

'I have to find out how to stop the homunculus growth in the three of you,' Toshiko said weakly. 'If we leave it too long you'll die. Or at least Ianto and Owen will. Who knows how it will affect you?'

Jack shrugged, and Owen said, 'So leave her to get on with it, if you don't mind...'

Jack nodded at the monitor showing Gwen and Saskia. 'What's going on with those two? Can we get sound?'

Ianto reached over and pressed a switch, and Gwen's voice was channelled through the speaker system.

'I'm not scared of you,' Gwen said.

Saskia smiled. 'Yes you are. I can see you trembling.'

'I'm ill.'

'I know. But don't worry. It'll soon be all over.'

There was a tiny crackle in Gwen's ear. She tried not to

flinch as she heard Ianto's voice. 'Gwen. We can hear every word. But listen – Tosh is all right. I repeat, she's all right.'

Then, before she could take the news in, she heard Jack's voice. He sounded tired and weak, almost unrecognisable as his words slurred into her ear: 'Tosh isn't infected, Gwen, and neither are you. It doesn't affect women. Only us guys.' There was a long, scraping cough. 'Man flu, eh?'

Gwen smiled, and stood a little straighter. Her hand moved behind her back and gripped the butt of her gun.

'Naughty,' said Saskia warningly.

'I said I'm not scared of you,' Gwen said, lifting the automatic out and levelling it at the woman. It took all of Gwen's nerve to keep the heavy pistol from wavering. She felt like she was shaking inside but she had to keep the gun still. She sighted carefully along the barrel, training the little metal V at the front of the gun on Saskia's pale forehead. 'I'm not scared,' she repeated.

Saskia simply smiled, and Gwen felt a cold touch on her neck as long, clawed fingers slowly wrapped themselves around her throat.

She'd been grabbed from behind. The long, twig-like fingers encircled her neck and squeezed. It felt like a cold, wet rope being pulled taut and she simply stopped breathing.

Another hand reached around from behind her and deftly removed the gun from her weakened hands. Gwen felt utterly unable to resist as all the strength seemed to drain out of her feet. All she could do was watch, dumbly, unable to even draw breath, as the green hand with its long, ragged claws removed the automatic from sight.

Whatever had hold of her from behind now stepped closer, moving its body against hers, bringing its mouth right next to her ear so that she could feel its cold, stinking breath on her face.

'Surprise,' it said.

TWENTY-FOUR

'Water hag,' said Jack, pointing at the screen.

His finger was resting on the fuzzy image of a tall, skeletal figure with long, dark hair standing behind Gwen, relieving her of her gun. The pistol was casually tossed away, irrelevant, forgotten. Gwen seemed to be sinking as they watched, her knees giving way.

'It's the one Bob Strong coughed up,' Owen said. 'Fully grown. It has to be. Saskia's not working on her own.'

'We've got to help Gwen,' croaked Ianto, moving towards the lift. He collapsed halfway, sliding down the concrete steps until he hit the floor with a clang. He lay there and coughed, bringing up red slime and heaving as he felt the homunculus inside him quiver in anticipation.

'That is what these things grow into, isn't it?' Jack said, tapping the image on the monitor. 'Water hags.'

Toshiko shook her head as she worked hurriedly at the keyboard. 'I've no idea what they're really called, but yes, these are the creatures that have been living in stagnant ponds and lakes – dragging people to their deaths, killing, preparing the way…'

Owen lifted his head heavily, blinking. 'Preparing the way for what?'

'Invasion.'

Jack nodded, pushing himself upright so he could look at the images on the other screens, where Toshiko had pulled up a map of the region peppered with blinking green dots. 'Yeah. This is it. The first sightings were all way out, in canals and rivers and ponds and marshland, in a huge circle around Cardiff. But they've been getting closer, drawing in all the time…'

'Homing in on the Rift,' realised Toshiko.

'Spreading the disease on the way. Releasing the spores, infecting every human who breathes 'em in.'

Owen stood up shakily. 'But only the men produce a new one, right? It grows inside them, then climbs out, ready to turn into one of them. A snotty little water hag.'

'And so it goes on.' Toshiko said. 'An exponential cycle.'

More green dots appeared on the screen. Clustered in the heart of Cardiff. A few keystrokes zoomed in on the city centre, showing a cluster of dots all around the bay. 'They're everywhere.'

'They're coming for the Rift,' Jack said, falling heavily against the railing again and sliding to the floor. 'Gwen? Gwen, can you hear me…?'

'All right, what's going on here, ladies? It's not Hallowe'en yet, y'know.'

The policeman smiled happily, thumbs hooked into his belt, pleased at his joke. Gwen sagged, and she knew that he would presume she was drunk. The cop duly ignored her, dismissing her as a likely threat, and turned his attention to her mate in the fancy dress.

His face fell when he looked into her eyes. 'Crikey,' he whispered. 'That's enough to give anyone a bad turn, that, love.' He recovered slightly and grinned again. 'You'll be giving me nightmares!'

Gwen tried to raise a hand to point at the water fountain behind him, but she barely had the strength.

But when Saskia Harden, who had been observing all this with amusement, finally spoke, the result was almost comic. 'It's all right, officer,' she said. 'These are my friends. It's a private party.'

The policeman whirled round and stared at her, blinking. 'Pardon me, miss,' he stammered. 'I didn't see you there. Bloody hell, I must be blind! You lot been to this party, then, or just going? Hen night, is it?'

Saskia stepped off the pavement, walking slowly towards the policeman. Gwen wanted to warn him, to tell him to run, but all she could do was open her mouth and watch.

'See,' continued the policeman, smiling politely at Saskia as she approached, 'you can't actually hang around here any longer, girls. With all this business with the bug that's going round, we've got to keep people on the streets to an absolute minimum. Orders, see. Everyone indoors.'

'I quite understand, officer,' said Saskia. 'I'm not sure my friends will, though.'

'Eh?' The policeman turned around to see a number of equally strange women walking across the area towards them. They were all moving at the same pace, converging on the water tower. 'Hello, girls.'

They drew closer, and the policeman had to squint at some of them as they approached. They all appeared to be wearing masks – white faces with thin, viciously sharp features and long, straggling wet hair. There was something in the hair – weeds or grass, he couldn't tell in the dark. 'Boy, you're a scary lot. Wouldn't like to meet you on a dark night.'

'You just have,' said Saskia.

They watched it on the CCTV monitor. One of the water hags reached out with long, sharp fingers and tore away the policeman's throat. He lurched back, a jet of blood visible in the air for a moment before he simply corkscrewed to the ground and lay there, kicking and waving while they gathered round and watched.

Jack used the last of his strength to pull himself up by Toshiko's chair. 'Got to stop them…'

Toshiko turned and looked at him. He was ashen-faced, his eyes bloodshot and hooded. As he spoke, blood appeared on his white lips. 'You can barely stand,' she told him, her voice hollow. 'You can't fight.'

'Gotta do something…' He sank back down to his knees, hands falling limply. 'What's happening to me… Why am I so weak?'

Toshiko looked at him, and at the others: Owen, propped up against the wall by the sofa, wracked by coughs, holding his chest and throat. Ianto, sprawled on the floor below them, weeping and gurgling through the massive build-up of mucus.

Toshiko looked back at her computers, at the keyboards. Her hands were shaking, but she knew she had no choice. 'The homunculi are getting ready to hatch,' she told Jack, trying to sound matter-of-fact, as scientific as possible. Not as though she was terrified out of her wits. 'They're growing fast and taking all the energy they need from you. That's why you're so weak.'

'Right,' Jack said. 'We need to get rid of them. How?'

'I'm not sure. I can think of a few things that might work, but it's not certain—'

'Do it,' Jack urged her weakly, screwing his face up in pain. 'Do 'em all. Anything.'

'It might not work. It might kill you.'

He opened his eyes and stared up at her. 'Wanna bet?'

The policeman gradually stopped moving. It was a slow process. Gwen watched him die, watched the lifeblood running out of his neck and across the flagstones, winding its way through the cracks in little geometric red rivers. There was nothing she could do to prevent it.

Eventually the man's legs stopped quivering and all was quiet. The hags had done nothing but stand over him and watch, silent and patient. Now some of them reached down to dip their long, crooked fingers into the blood, lifting it to their lips.

Gwen started to crawl away, tears running down her face. She didn't get far before one of the water hags picked her up as if she weighed nothing. Gwen felt her feet leave the ground and she hung in the air while Saskia approached. 'Going somewhere?'

'You're sick,' Gwen spat at her. 'Twisted!'

'I'm afraid not. We're just survivors, like you. Only we're better at it, obviously.'

The water hag let her go and Gwen crashed to the ground,

crying out in pain. She rolled over and away, but she couldn't get far. She was just too weak. She crawled another metre or so and then stopped, coughing heavily, and Saskia laughed. 'And by the way, you're the one who's sick, remember?'

'Why here?' Gwen asked, panting. 'Why Earth?'

'Why not?'

'Because we're here. The human race. It's our planet.'

'Not for much longer.'

Gwen smiled and gave a little laugh, sinking to her knees.

'What's so funny?' Saskia demanded.

'Nothing. It's just…' Gwen laughed again. 'It's just… I can't believe aliens are invading Earth… starting with Cardiff.'

'I'm glad you find it so amusing.'

Gwen stopped laughing, straightened her face, bit her lip. 'No, no, you're right, it's not funny,' she said. 'But this is.'

She brought the gun up, pulled the trigger. The shot echoed around the bay area, the muzzle flash lighting up the water tower like a camera flash. Saskia jerked backwards, lifted off her feet by the bullet. It probably wasn't a killing shot. She hadn't been able to take her time and aim properly. She had just managed to crawl her way over to where the gun had been lying half-hidden in the shadow of the tower, and grab it, shoot it. But it was enough. The other water hags hissed in shock, automatically turning to their leader as she staggered backwards.

And then Gwen ran, heading for the road, pointing the automatic behind her and pulling the trigger again and again. She didn't care if she hit any of them, she just wanted to create a noise, a commotion, something that would attract attention. She couldn't do this on her own.

Toshiko slid the needle deep into Jack's forearm and depressed the plunger. The contents of the syringe disappeared into his bloodstream as she looked up at him and smiled. 'Just a little prick,' she said with a shy smile.

'Knew you'd say that,' he croaked. He tried returning the smile but didn't really have the strength. Instead he closed his eyes and sank back into his office chair with a sigh.

Toshiko bit her lip. She looked at the empty hypodermic thoughtfully.

'What was in it?' asked Owen. He had crawled across the floor, coughing fitfully and too weak to stand up. His eyes were red-rimmed, the skin around them a distinct grey colour. He knew, as Toshiko did, that every time he coughed now could be the beginning of the end. His lips were caked in thick, congealing blood.

'It's a cocktail,' she told him. 'A wide-spectrum antibiotic mixed with an emetic and a little something extra.'

'Antibiotics are a long shot,' whispered Owen. 'Emetics won't help. What's the little extra?'

'Oestrogen.'

As sick as he was, Owen still managed to raise an eyebrow. 'Female hormones? Jack will be delighted.'

Toshiko looked back at Jack. He hadn't moved and his breathing was shallow. He was paler than ever, deep shadows around his eyes and his cheeks sunken. She had never seen him look so bad.

'I'm hoping the mixture will be enough to weaken the homunculus and cause it to exit early. That way it might not kill the host.'

With an effort Owen levered himself up on one arm and began to roll up his sleeve. 'Give it to me as well.'

'I can't,' Toshiko said. 'It's purely experimental. Jack's taking the risk for you.'

'Tosh… we can't afford to wait…' Owen was breathing with difficulty now, forcing air in and out of his lungs in huge, wheezing gulps. 'If Jack can take his chances… then so must we.'

Toshiko helped him upright. 'It's a one in three chance of success, Owen. Not great odds.'

'One in three? I'd call that perfect odds. Jack, Ianto and me. One of us will make it.' Owen coughed, retching on his hands and knees, putting one hand up to his neck as the muscles bulged until the veins stood out like wires.

'Everybody…' Ianto's voice, although small and weak, nevertheless carried right across the Hub. Perhaps it was the note of alarm that attracted their attention, but Toshiko and Owen both turned around to look at him. Ianto was leaning against Toshiko's workstation, pointing at one of the CCTV monitors.

Toshiko hurried across for a closer look. 'It's Gwen,' she said. The screen showed Gwen backing away from the water tower, gun in hand, surrounded by water hags.

Owen pulled himself up onto the seat. Jack was still unconscious, his head lolling back, exposing the skin of his throat. The flesh was moving as the homunculus inside began to stir.

'It's starting,' Owen said.

TWENTY-FIVE

Gwen didn't have nearly enough ammunition to shoot her way out of this kind of trouble. She counted half a dozen water hags in front of her, and, flicking her head around, counted another four or five behind her. They were closing in, slowly, inexorably. Their long, bony fingers waved slowly, vicious claws glinting in the moonlight.

Where was everybody? Where were the cops? Never around when you needed them!

The water hags in front of her parted and Saskia Harden walked through. There was a bullet hole in her raincoat, on the right-hand side, just underneath where her collarbone should be. There was some kind of dark stain seeping through the material around the hole, but it wasn't blood. It was a deep, inky green colour. As she approached, she unbelted the raincoat and let it slip from her shoulders with a casual shrug.

She was naked beneath. She took three more steps and then, passing through a shadow, her body seemed to ripple slightly. Gwen stared as she walked back into the light of the street lamps and then, with sudden clarity, realised what was happening. Saskia was shucking her human disguise like she had her raincoat.

At first, it looked as though water was streaming over her skin, running down her face and body as if she was standing under a shower. The shimmering passed over her like a sudden glimpse of silver scales, a fish-like iridescence that coursed through her features, robbing them of all humanity, flowing down between her breasts and out beneath the rest of her skin. She darkened, quickly and permanently, as if she was burning up without any visible flames, the flesh crisping into a rough, gnarled texture full of cracks and fissures.

'Keep back,' Gwen said, her voice firm as she carefully aimed her gun. She felt as if, finally confronted with the hideous wrongness, a preternatural resolve was flooding through her. She wouldn't go down without a fight. 'I swear I'll shoot if you take another step.'

The water hag smiled. Or at least that's what Gwen thought it must have been doing. She could see a lot of teeth, but its facial expressions failed to correspond with anything Gwen recognised. All her natural, instinctive behavioural cues were missing. With dreadful fascination, Gwen realised that she was looking right into the eyes of a truly alien being.

The eyes were narrow, pus-yellow, with latitudinal slits like those of a goat. They were set deep in the face, surrounded by a thick web of shadows. The nose was little more than a jutting blade surmounting vertical holes like those in a skull. Beneath this was the wide, crescent-shaped mouth, parted to show the grey, needle-like teeth and a thin, flickering black tongue.

And when the smile came – and now Gwen knew it *was* a smile – the thin lipless crack opened wider and wider until the horrible teeth seemed to reach right up to where the ears should be. If Saskia yawned now, Gwen thought, the entire top half of her head would tip back on a hinge. No wonder she could bite the head off a dog.

It was, quite simply, the smile of death.

Gwen held her ground, kept the pistol aimed levelly. She held it in a two-handed grip, sighting down the barrel until she was sure the next shot would go straight through the water hag's forehead.

'Don't be frightened,' Saskia said. Her voice was low, rippling, as if she was speaking underwater. Her once blonde hair now hung like seaweed around her head.

'I'm not frightened,' Gwen said. She hoped she sounded more convinced about that than she felt. Now that she was closer, Gwen could see that the water hag's skin was full of mud and moss and crawling with tiny worms and insects. The dark yellow eyes never left hers.

'Of course you are. But you can relax. I'm not going to kill you. I need you alive.'

Somehow that sounded far worse than a simple threat to kill her. Gwen couldn't feel her fingers any longer, and the gun was slipping in her grip as her hands perspired. She could feel her heart beating so hard that her pulse had to be visible in her neck.

The other water hags were much closer now. Gwen could smell them all around her, the stench of something wet and rotting. She couldn't kill all of them. Even if she shot Saskia, how would she get the others? They'd rip her throat out before she could do anything.

'W-what are you, really? Where are you from?'

'Here and there. A world a long way from here, originally.'

Keep her talking. 'What was it called?'

'Strepto. Not that it matters much. It's disappeared, vanished. I was away, travelling. When I went home it was gone. So I came here on my own, the last survivor.'

'On your own?'

'At first. Not any more.'

'What d'you want?' Gwen was gripping the automatic ever more tightly, keeping the heavy gun – it was so heavy – trained on Saskia's forehead.

'We need to get in there,' Saskia replied, pointing down at the ground.

The Hub. Where Jack and the others all lay dying.

Saskia took another step closer. The muzzle of Gwen's gun was no more than thirty centimetres from her head now. 'My turn to ask the questions now. What's your name?'

'Gwen.'

'You're going to take me in there, Gwen. I'm not interested in you or your friends, but I need what you've got down there.'

'You won't get it.'

'I think I will. With your help.'

'I'll shoot you dead and take my chances. You're not getting into the Hub.'

'Are you sure about that?'

Gwen gripped the pistol tighter. 'Try me.'

'Pulling that trigger will be the last thing you ever do, Gwen.'

Gwen's mouth felt so dry she could hardly speak. 'And watching me do it will be the last thing you ever do.'

Saskia took another step closer.

'I'm warning you!' Gwen shouted.

Saskia smiled.

This was it, Gwen realised. The final act of her life. Her heart was pounding so hard it hurt in her chest, hurt deep inside her stomach. She felt like she wanted to just stop and cry, but she knew that she couldn't. This was the final act. She thought of Tosh, clever and gentle Tosh, and the talk they'd had in the motorway services, of Professor Len, and Rhys. Tears were running down her face and she knew she was incapable of speaking now. There was only one thing left to do. She said a silent, choking goodbye to Rhys and pulled the trigger.

TWENTY-SIX

Click.

For a long, long moment, nobody moved. There was complete silence. Gwen was faintly aware of the water in the bay, and then the feel of the wind on her face, and the sad, condescending smile on Saskia's hideous face.

'Whoops,' she said gently. 'Gun empty. Never mind.'

And, in a flash, the water hag's long arm shot out, and the hooked talons on the end of her fingers raked the pistol out of Gwen's hands. The gun spun through the air, away into the darkness, to land with a distant, irrelevant clatter.

Gwen looked with incomprehension at her hands. Saskia's claws had ripped the underside of her left hand wide open and blood was pouring down her wrists, dripping onto the pavement at her feet in big red blotches.

Then her legs gave way, knees dropping, and she fell with a dry croak to the floor.

Only to be picked up by Saskia again and dangled in the air. 'Oh no,' she said. 'It's not time for you to go yet, Gwen.

You're my key to the Rift…' She raised Gwen a little higher and then dipped her head so that she could lick the blood from her hand with her long, black tongue. 'Mmm. Yummy humans.'

'Bitch,' said Gwen.

'You know, I have to say I'm a little disappointed. I'd heard it said that Earth was defended.' Saskia gave a light chuckle. 'Is this really all you've got?'

'Not quite,' said a voice from behind her.

Saskia twisted her head at an unnatural angle to see who had spoken. Gwen could just see the figure stepping out of the shadows by the wharf. The lights from the bay cast a soft halo around the outline of a tall man in a long coat.

'There's always me,' said Jack. He raised his arm and aimed his revolver at the water hag. The other aliens turned and hissed like frightened cats, but Saskia seemed unmoved.

'Captain Harkness,' she purred. 'How nice to see you again. And looking so well.'

'Touch of flu,' Jack said. 'Over it now.'

Saskia frowned. 'No unexpected arrivals? No pitter-patter of tiny feet?'

'Oh, yeah, there was that.' Jack pulled a face and then lifted his leg, holding up his foot so that Saskia could see the bottom of his boot. There were lumps of blood and flesh jammed into the rugged treads. 'Had to put my foot down, though.'

Saskia glared fiercely at the remains but said nothing.

'I missed you in the park,' Jack continued, narrowing his eyes as he took careful aim. 'But I won't miss now.'

Saskia swung Gwen around until she was dangling in front of her, protecting her. 'Want to bet?'

'Human shield, huh?' Jack tutted. 'You guys never learn.'

And then he pulled the trigger.

Gwen felt the heat of the bullet as it passed her face. Her skin was scorched, but she only became aware of the pain after she'd heard the heavy thud of the round hitting Saskia. The water hag was knocked backwards, but she kept her grip on Gwen's throat and brought her down on top of her. Gwen landed awkwardly, unable to break her fall, but satisfied in that all of her weight had come down on the water hag's chest. There was a gust of cold, fetid air as the breath was knocked out of her. Gwen twisted, struggling, but Saskia maintained her grip, the stick-like fingers closing tighter around her neck, threatening to suffocate her. Gwen's struggles grew more panicky as she realised that she really couldn't breathe; and she was more frightened by that than the green ichor spurting all over her from the wound in Saskia's neck.

Then someone grabbed her by the scruff, wrenched her aside so violently that Saskia almost ripped her head off, and jammed an old service revolver into the water hag's face.

'Did I mention what a good shot I am?' asked Jack. His finger squeezed the trigger, but the shot, at point-blank range, exploded into the ground beneath as Saskia slammed him aside using Gwen as a bludgeon. The two of them sprawled across the concrete, then Saskia leapt to her feet, still holding on to Gwen. Jack turned onto his back, bringing the pistol up, but suddenly the water hag held the high ground.

'Not good enough,' Saskia hissed, throwing Gwen down on top of him.

Gwen gasped, choking and retching as she tried to draw breath, aware of the searing pain in her left hand more than anything else. Jack rolled, trying to free himself, but the advantage was lost. The other water hags, at a signal from

225

their leader, were closing in, claws and teeth bared. Jack couldn't shoot them all, no matter how good a shot he was.

There was a moment of stalemate: Gwen on all fours, barely able to breathe; Jack on one knee beside her, hand on her shoulder, his gun raised, sweeping it back and forth across the approaching aliens.

'Who's gonna be first to die?' he asked savagely.

'Does it matter?' Saskia responded. 'You have four bullets left. There's eight of us here – and how many more are due to arrive in the next day or so? A hundred? A thousand?'

'They'll never make it,' Jack told her. 'We've got the antidote. There's a serum which will kill the homunculi in situ. I've got my people working on it now, transmitting the formula to the authorities. By morning, they'll be rolling it out right across the country. Kills 'em dead.'

Saskia bared her black fangs. 'Is that what you did to yours?'

'Coughed it right up on the floor and then squashed it under my boot,' Jack growled.

'No mercy?'

'Not when the planet's at stake. This is Torchwood. We don't do political correctness.'

'Then you'll understand that I can't show you any mercy in return,' Saskia smiled. 'As you say, not when the planet's at stake. You die and the Earth is ours.'

'And that's where we come in,' said Owen Harper.

He was standing away to one side, with Ianto right beside him. Even in the moonlight, Gwen could see that neither of them looked well – white-faced, haggard, almost at the point of collapse. They were armed with sub-machine guns but, even so, as a rescue attempt she had to admit it didn't look promising. Owen was leaning against the wall in order to remain upright, lips pressed into a thin line, the Heckler & Koch MP5 tucked in against his waist as if it was too heavy to hold properly. Ianto, unbelievably, was in shirtsleeves – bloodstained and open-necked, and, clutching the gun, looking more like an extra from a *Die Hard* film than an immaculate butler.

'I think the saying is, "Put your hands up",' said Ianto.

'Don't listen to him,' Owen cut in. 'Believe me, I want to shoot.'

Moving as one, the water hags screamed and flew into action. Several dived towards Owen and Ianto, claws slashing, but the response was never in doubt: the MP5s roared and the hags were cut down in mid air, spraying dark blood into the night.

Next, confusion: Gwen crawling out of the way, dimly aware that Jack was moving in the opposite direction. More water hags yelling and hissing, and frequent, controlled bursts of gunfire from the SMGs. Gwen looked back at one point and saw Owen standing over a fallen water hag, MP5 directed at its head, execution-style. One point-blank burst shattered the head like a dropped melon and he moved on, face grim.

Ianto was down on one knee, his own weapon raised to his shoulder so that he could aim more carefully. He, too, was squeezing off short, shattering rounds, picking off the water hags where they stood. The one nearest to Gwen was flung back in a hail of gunfire. Weed and moss slopped onto the pavement as the creature staggered back and fell. It crawled along the pavement trailing weeds and green slime, whining to itself, but still very much alive.

Toshiko's voice flooded into Gwen's head: 'Gwen, can you read me?'

'Yeah, I'm here.'

'Thank goodness you're all right. I'm checking the CCTV – Saskia's heading for the quay.'

Gwen twisted around, peering past the wounded hag lying on the ground nearby, through the gun smoke drifting across Roald Dahl Plass, and saw Saskia disappearing into the darkness towards the bay – closely followed by a tall, running figure in a greatcoat.

'Jack's after her,' said Gwen.

'I think she's heading for the water,' Toshiko said. 'Safety, as far as she's concerned… Cardiff Bay is fresh water, not sea water. Gwen, she mustn't get there.'

'I'm on it.' Gwen heaved herself upright, holding her injured hand under the opposite arm, trying to ignore the sharp waves of pain bursting through the lacerated flesh. She tried to keep low, running in a crouch in the hope of avoiding any stray bullets.

Ianto had taken cover behind a bench, firing at the remaining water hags, trying to hold them off. No matter how many carefully aimed shots he used, they refused to die. 'Alien anatomy,' Ianto muttered in disgust as he hurriedly snapped a fresh magazine into the H&K. 'You can never be sure which bit to shoot at, can you?'

Gwen stepped over the bench and dropped down beside him. 'Jack's gone after Saskia,' she said. 'Can you hold them here?'

Ianto nodded. 'I can try. No promises, mind.'

Gwen nodded, got up and ran down towards the sea front.

'Which way did they go?' she asked Toshiko.

'Down towards Mermaid Quay, I think. They're in a CCTV black spot. I've lost them both.'

Gwen swore and hurried on. The pain in her hand was terrible now, a momentous throb of agony that kept distracting her. She stopped, hunched over, fighting back the urge to sob and wail, knowing she had to concentrate and do the job. But she could hardly move for the pain; she could hardly think.

She stumbled on a few paces. 'Jack? Jack, are you here?'

There was no reply except for the sound of the water washing against the quayside. She slumped down against the side of the building, feeling cold and utterly alone. Her hand was burning, but she was starting to shiver as the cold wind came in off the bay and cut right through her denim jacket.

'Jack?' she called out again, but her voice sounded very small and the word was carried away into the night by the wind.

Slowly she lifted a hand to her ear. 'Tosh? Toshiko? Are you there?'

Silence.

TWENTY-SEVEN

She heard footsteps pounding along the boardwalk and opened her eyes to see Owen arrive, breathing hard. 'What's going on?'

'Jack's after Saskia,' Gwen told him faintly. 'Tosh saw them heading for the waterfront. I can't find them, and now I can't get a reply from Tosh either. What's happening?'

Owen collapsed next to her against the Tourist Information kiosk, his breath coming in harsh, ugly gasps. 'Dunno. The water hags won't stay down when we shoot 'em. How unfair is that? Ianto's trying to pin them back, but he won't be able to keep it going for ever.'

'We're stuffed, aren't we?'

He rested his head against the wood and closed his eyes. 'Give me a second and then I'll try to find Jack. He might know what to do.'

'Stay here, you're done in,' advised Gwen.

'What about you?' he panted, nodding at her hand. 'You're injured.'

'It's nothing, I'll live.'

Owen shook his head. There was too much blood. When Gwen glanced down she saw that her T-shirt was soaked in it and the sight almost made her faint.

'Let me see it,' Owen said, dropping his MP5 on the ground.

Carefully, Gwen pulled her hand out from under her arm. The blood had started to congeal and her T-shirt stuck momentarily to the flesh, making her gasp as it came free.

Owen already had his medical kit out, unwrapping a field dressing with trembling fingers. Gwen cried out as her turned her hand over, examining the deep cut along the edge with a tut. 'Nasty. Could've been worse – missed an artery by half an inch.'

'Funnily enough, that doesn't make me feel any better…'

Owen pressed the dressing against the wound and then began to wind adhesive tape around it. 'This'll stop it bleeding, but you're going to need stitches.' He looked up at her and smiled coldly. 'For you, my dear, ze var is over.'

'What about you? What happened down in the Hub?'

Owen avoided her eyes then, looking quickly down at her hand as he worked. The smile faded. 'Tosh came up with a serum – some sort of vaccine. God knows what she was thinking of, she's no doctor. Educated guess, I suppose – and the best person for it. Made the homunculi emerge early.'

Gwen watched his face carefully. It was twitching in a way she knew only too well – Owen was being forced into talking about something he didn't want to even think about.

He still wouldn't look at her as he fished out a morphine syrette from his kit, pulled the cap off with his teeth and jabbed it quickly and expertly into her arm.

'Ow,' she said.

'Painkiller.'

'You could have fooled me.'

'Always do.'

'What happened to the homunculi?'

Owen stopped for a moment, hesitated, and then packed away the rest of the medical kit. 'Dead.'

Gwen thought back to Jack, raising his boot so that Saskia could see the bloody detritus in the treads. She felt sick.

'Still,' Owen said, finally looking up at her and rewarding her with that sudden, cheeky smile, 'Better out than in, eh?'

'Saskia Harden!'

They heard Jack's voice calling out from somewhere behind them. Owen helped Gwen up, and together they limped down to the quayside.

Further along, next to the railings overlooking the bay, stood Jack. His coat swirled in the freezing wind coming in off the water, but otherwise he stood rock still, as if he was challenging the elements themselves.

Of Saskia there was no sign – until a dark blur appeared out of the night air and struck Jack square in the chest, lifting him right off his feet. He hit the ground and rolled, coming up on all fours, ready for the next assault.

The water hag leapt on him with a savage growl, talons raking the air, missing him by a fraction of an inch as Jack twisted away, but not quickly enough – the next slashing sweep caught him on the shoulder and tore right through the heavy material of his greatcoat.

He used the impact to dive further, hit the ground again and jumped to his feet. At the same time, he threw off the greatcoat, wrapping it around one forearm as a bulky shield

233

to absorb the next lash with the talons. He just about made it, as Saskia was on him with another series of wild, flailing attempts to rip his head clean off.

Eventually, Jack was able to drop his body, swinging his boot up so that it connected with the water hag's throat and sent her flying backwards. Jack stumbled, shirt hanging in tatters off one arm, blood running down from his shoulder. Saskia rounded on him again, exchanging furious blows and snarls, until Jack swung under one of the swinging claws, punched her hard in the kidney area, and then flung her in a judo throw high over his shoulder to land with a splintering crash on the boardwalk.

Saskia scrambled back onto her feet, eyes blazing, but stationary.

Jack stood, his shirt in shreds, blood streaming from multiple cuts and slashes over his shoulders, chest and face.

For a minute, the two of them stood where they had landed, glaring at each other, waiting to see who would make the next move. Jack was panting hard but Saskia still looked fresh. Then her grey-green flesh suddenly rippled, and she resumed her appearance as a striking blonde human woman.

A striking, blonde, naked human woman.

'Oh, I bet you do that to all the boys,' said Jack. Even from behind, Gwen could tell in his voice that he'd summoned that boyish grin of his, the one that, combined with his looks and blue eyes, could charm a nun out of her habit.

'By the way,' Jack continued, beginning to get his breath back, 'Saskia Harden or Sally Blackteeth? If we're gonna get to know each other better, I need to know which one is your real name.'

'Neither.' She started to walk towards him, controlled,

poised. Ready for the contest.

'I bet your real name's unpronounceable by human beings,' Jack said. 'They usually are.'

Saskia spat something which sounded like a cross between a curse and someone choking on custard.

'Nice name,' Jack said. 'Prefer Saskia, though.'

She stopped short of him by just a couple of metres. 'So this is it, is it, Jack?'

He drew his revolver and pointed it at her head. 'Stay where you are.'

'Too close for comfort?'

'Close enough. I never kiss on a first date anyway.'

'So what are you going to do? Shoot me where I stand?'

'If I have to.' Jack let out a sigh, a tiny wisp of breath that disappeared on the breeze. 'But I'd rather give you the chance to leave. Just go.'

'That could be a problem.' She was standing so close to him now, her nakedness contrasting with his torn clothes and boots. 'I have nowhere else to go. I'm hopeless. Strepto is gone – just disappeared.'

Jack raised an eyebrow but said nothing.

'So it's Earth or nothing, I'm afraid.'

'It can't be Earth,' said Jack. 'So that leaves nothing.'

'Or somewhere in between,' Saskia replied. Then she simply turned, stepped up to the edge of the quay in one smooth motion and leapt out into the bay.

Jack roared, 'No!' He darted forward, just in time to see her disappear beneath the waves. Immediately he hurled his greatcoat away and removed his boots.

'Jack, don't be stupid!' yelled Gwen, catching up with him.

'She's gone! Let it go!' Owen added furiously.

Jack glanced back at them, just the once, and his eyes were ice cold. Then he turned, threw his arms above his head and dived off the quayside. He hit the churning water like an arrow and vanished beneath the dark, uncaring surface.

Gwen stared, open-mouthed. 'What did he do that for?'

'You know Jack,' Owen panted. 'Never gives up.'

'I can't see him anywhere!'

They watched the cold swell of the ocean but there was no sign of either Saskia or Jack.

'The currents are strong around here,' Owen said. 'They could've been dragged right down into the bay.'

They heard footsteps and turned to see Ianto coming up, Heckler & Koch slung over his shoulder. His face was smudged and dirty and his hair was a mess. 'It's no use,' he told them, his voice ragged. 'I couldn't hold them off. The bullets just wouldn't stop them.'

'Where are they now?' Owen asked.

'Heading for the water tower. They're circling it.' Ianto swallowed hard. 'Where's Jack?'

Gwen pointed out at the bay but, before Ianto could respond, Toshiko's voice came through: 'Everyone! Listen! We have an emergency in the Hub – repeat, an emergency in the Hub.'

'What's up?' Gwen asked.

'I think something's coming through the Rift,' Toshiko said. She was trying to keep calm, but there was no mistaking the shrill edge of panic in her voice. 'It's coming through right into the Hub. Lots of things... I can see something in the water... Oh no, they're in the water...'

'It's them,' Ianto said. 'The water hags. They've got inside the Hub.'

TWENTY-EIGHT

The water closed over his head like a coffin lid, shutting out every sight and sound.

It was cold, black, silent. For a few seconds, Jack let the current sweep him along, turning him over and over, letting the icy grasp of the water wash away the blood and the fear. Then, catching sight of a lithe, blonde figure in the darkness beneath him, Jack started to move. With strong, urgent strokes he pulled himself deeper, ignoring the flurry of weed and debris which caught in his arms and legs.

Saskia swam deeper, using a strange, alien motion reminiscent of an eel. Her blonde hair transformed into long, trailing weeds, and her skin took on its native, muddy texture.

Jack followed her, lungs and muscles aching as he hauled himself further down. She was disappearing into the murk. If he didn't keep up, he would lose her for ever. Teeth gritted, he swam harder, aware that it was getting colder and colder the deeper they went. If he drowned down here, what would happen? The current would take him, wash him up some place, leave him to choke and gasp like a landed fish until life flooded back into him yet again. There would be no escape for him down here; but he wouldn't let Saskia escape either.

He found her floating in front of him. She loomed out of the darkness like the ghost of a drowned woman, her hair waving around her head like a living thing, part blonde, part weed. Her face was human and beautiful – until she smiled, revealing a mouthful of hundreds of sharp, needle teeth.

She grabbed him, pulled him closer as if she was going to kiss him, jaws opening like those of a shark. Jack lashed out, grabbing her around the throat before she could bite, pushing her back, trying to keep her at arm's length.

A plume of bubbles broke from his lips as Saskia whipped back and forth, trying to break his grip. Jack swallowed water, clamped his lips shut, pulled back his fist and tried to break her jaw. But he couldn't fight properly underwater. No one could.

No one except a water hag, a creature born to live in the water as easily as out of it. A creature infamous for luring innocent humans underwater, dragging them down to their deaths.

They pelted down the secret passageway leading from the Tourist Information kiosk, through the giant cog-wheel door, the flashing lights, the holding cage. The Hub looked all wrong. The main lights were down, and there was a dull green glow reflected from the tiled surfaces and metal walkways. In the centre of the Hub stood the base of the water tower fountain, strange, multicoloured lights shimmering across the surface.

Toshiko was sitting at her workstation, where the screens showed a series of wildly fluctuating blue patterns, overwritten by computer graphics and equations. The others knew just enough to tell that the readings weren't good.

Gwen, Ianto and Owen all crowded around Toshiko, peering at the screens, firing questions.

'I don't know,' Toshiko stammered. 'It's been fluctuating for some time, but this is a sudden change. Like nothing I've seen before – not even when the Rift was opened. This is different – as if the Rift itself is… reacting.'

'Reacting to what?' asked Owen.

'Take a look,' Toshiko replied. 'At the tower.'

They all looked across at the silver monolith rising up in the centre of the Hub. Heliotropic lights swirled across the tower like oil mixed with the water which streamed down the mirrored surface, sending ripples out into the pool of water at its base. But there was something causing further ripples in the water which ran vertically down the tower, as if something invisible was disturbing the flow.

Owen and Ianto went down for a closer look. The water was trickling in specific patterns, making way for something they simply couldn't see until Ianto pointed, and said, 'Look – look at the shape the water's making…'

The water had bulged out as if running over a ball of air, but there were shapes in the bulge, moving, thrusting forward out of the mirror behind. A face – long, sharp, trailing weeds.

'Water hag,' breathed Owen.

There were faces appearing all over the tower, spectral faces haunting the mirror.

'How can we stop them?' asked Ianto.

'We can't,' Owen said, staring in fascinated horror as

239

the faces grew more pronounced, more definite. He found himself looking directly into the eyes of a water hag as it began to emerge with a distinct sucking noise.

'There may be a way,' Toshiko said. 'The water hags are all connected in some way – to the Rift, as we already know… but also to the first water hag to arrive on Earth.'

'Saskia,' said Ianto.

'I've traced the temporal web between all the creatures,' Toshiko confirmed, indicating a complex, ever-changing pattern on one of her computer monitors. 'They all lead to Saskia.'

'They are all her children on Earth,' Gwen realised. 'She said she was here first – the only survivor. This is her new generation. Preparing the way for takeover.'

Toshiko nodded. 'She used the Rift to travel to Earth. But it's not a reliable method of travel. She arrived back in the Middle Ages. She knew she had to find a way to procreate – to use human beings to create more of her kind.'

'Using coughs and sneezes,' Owen said. 'Reproduction via contagion.'

'But she was the first one, the progenitor. She came through the Rift, and is inextricably linked to the Rift, and thus all the other water hags are inextricably linked to her.'

'Which helps us how, exactly?' demanded Ianto. There was an edge of panic in his voice as he continued to watch the water hags materialising in the stream. 'What are they coming through here for? What do they want?'

'Control of the Rift?' suggested Toshiko. 'Perhaps they know about the Rift Manipulator. The reproduction by contagion is a bit hit-and-miss for invasion purposes. Control of the Rift could help.'

'What if it's control of us they want?' suggested Gwen. 'Control of Torchwood? They know we're the only people that can stop them.'

'*Were* the only people,' Owen corrected. 'Past tense.'

'Jack would know what to do,' said Ianto.

'Jack's not here!' Gwen yelled at him.

He was practically blind now. They were so deep and the water was so black and murky that he couldn't see his own hands, or the face of the creature in front of him. They were locked in a tight embrace, each trying to squeeze the life from the other, to exploit a moment of weakness neither would allow the other to sense.

Jack felt his grip on her loosening. His fingers, cold and rigid with the effort, had long since lost any sense of feeling, but he could tell, nevertheless, that she was slipping from his grasp. It was almost as if she was dissolving before him, the constituent parts of her breaking away and turning to liquid as they fought. And then, quite suddenly, there was nothing in his arms except water and a residual cloud of mud and blood.

He panicked. He was utterly disorientated, unable to tell what was up or down or how deep he was. If he tried swimming in any direction it could be the wrong one, taking him down further. But to allow himself to go limp, to hope that he would eventually float to the surface, would be to accept defeat. Saskia hadn't simply dissolved. She'd escaped.

And then there was the current, the deep swell beneath the waves that could suck him down, deeper and deeper and further away from the shore. He could feel it now, tugging at him, rippling through the freezing water all around him, clawing and dragging at him. And, in a distant part of his own mind, now as dark and cold as the water which surrounded him, he could hear the mad screech of laughter.

The tower was a mass of churning water and slime. The hags were forcing their way through the Rift, right at its very core, taking on solid form as the water cascaded around them. Particles of sand and mud and a thick syrup of mucus were combining in the torrent, clumping together to form faces and hands, arms and bodies.

'They *do* want the Rift Manipulator,' Toshiko realised. 'They want to open the Rift right up, use it to tear the world apart so they can rebuild it for themselves.'

'Get the guns,' said Owen, heading for the armoury.

'It's no use,' Ianto roared. 'It won't stop them, not for long enough.'

A large pustule of mud and seething matter bulged from the centre of the tower and suddenly unfolded long, angular legs like a giant insect emerging from its chrysalis. The limbs were a gnarled, twisted coagulate of mucus and soil, skinned by the moss and lichen which had covered the base of the tower, streaming with filthy water.

A head emerged, the face carved into a hideous mask full of sucking orifices and sharp black teeth like nails. Glowing spots opened up across the lump of matter, blinking yellow, like eyes emerging from the dark.

'What is it?' Gwen asked weakly, staggered by the overwhelming sense of wrongness which surrounded it. It shouldn't be here, not just in the Hub, but in her world. Alien was too small a word for it. It was an unnatural imposition on the Earth, an infected scab on the surface of her planet.

Toshiko swallowed, unable to take her eyes off the creature as it fought its way into existence via the Rift. She could hear alarm signals blaring and see, in the corner of her eye, the madly flickering images on her workstation as it monitored the process. Every sensor she had trained on the Rift was jangling. The Rift was being abused; forced to vomit this abhorrence into time and space.

'Look!' Ianto pointed, quite suddenly, his arm held out like a signpost. His eyes were wide, fixed on the disturbance at the base of the tower as the creature struggled madly out of its spatio-temporal womb.

There was something else with the creature. A figure clinging to its back like a rider on a runaway horse. Dark hair plastered to his head, white teeth bared with primeval effort. Arms clad in the tatters of a blue, soaking shirt were being wrapped around the creature's head.

'Jack,' said Gwen disbelievingly.

'It's Saskia!' Jack bellowed, digging his fingers into the craggy hide beneath him. The skin of the creature was not yet fully hardened. The carapace cracked beneath him and his fingers touched the cold jelly inside. 'It's Saskia!'

Owen picked up his gun, aiming with a certain, two-handed grip. His limbs felt a surge of strength and purpose. He pumped round after round into the exposed throat, walking towards it step by step, gaining confidence with every bubbling squeal of pain it let out.

Gelatinous mucus welled out of the bullet holes as the leathery skin split and cracked under the assault. Jack shifted his position on the beast's shoulders, wrapping his arm tightly around the snarling, slavering head until he could start pulling backwards. He dug his feet and knees in and heaved.

243

The head was pulled back further and further, tearing the flesh at the neck where Owen's shots had already weakened it.

And then, in a rush, it came free. The throat split open, exposing the raw matter inside. Jack began to fall as the creature thrashed reflexively, but he kept hold of the thing's head as he went, wrenching it completely free. Trailing thick strands of mucus and congealed blood, Jack and the head hit the concrete floor with a sickening crunch.

The decapitated body shuddered and collapsed, falling back against the tower, legs quivering. Water flowed over it as the struggles grew more feeble, dissolving the areas less formed.

Gwen and Ianto ran over to help Jack. He was coughing up water while trying to climb to his feet.

'Stay there,' Gwen said. 'Lie down, lie down. It's all right…'

'No,' he said. 'No, I want to stand. Want to.'

With their help, he stood.

The water was running freely down the tower, undisturbed. There was no sign of any other water hag. The remains of Saskia Harden lay in a heap at the base, half-submerged in the swilling water in the basin. Long strands of mud and lumps of moss trailed away through the water as it began to disintegrate.

'Followed her,' gasped Jack, chest heaving. 'She came through the Rift. Hung on to her, let her drag me through in her wake. Had to kill her. Had to. Only chance.'

'Take it easy,' Gwen urged. 'You're in no state to talk.'

Owen handed Jack a metal flask and he sucked greedily from it for a moment, pushing his wet hair back from his face with his free hand. 'Had to do it, then, while she was reforming,' he continued. 'She was vulnerable. Only chance.'

'I can't believe it's over,' said Toshiko. She stepped down to survey the damage, reaching out to touch Jack on the arm.

'It's gone,' Jack nodded. 'For ever.'

Ianto peered at the floor. 'Made a heck of a mess, though.'

TWENTY-NINE

Later, when Gwen was inspecting the perfect white dressing that Owen had put on her hand and Toshiko was busy at her workstation, recalibrating the Rift monitors, it all seemed so quiet.

The Hub was nearly silent, except for the hum and bleep of the computers and the quiet trickle from the water tower.

With her good hand, Gwen speed-dialled Rhys on her mobile. He picked up straight away. 'Gwen? Where are you?'

'I'm OK,' she said, sidestepping the question only slightly. It was so good to hear his voice. She'd been bottling up the worry about him, and now she had to make sure he was all right. 'How are you? Is everything all right?'

'Yeah, I'm fine. Bit of a cold coming on, though, I think. Heater's not been working in the cabin. You?'

'I'm fine.'

'You been involved in all this epidemic emergency, then? Sounds like your sort of stuff.'

'Yeah, a bit.'

'Thought I had it for a while,' Rhys laughed. 'They're talking about a big immunisation programme on the news. The whole country – starting with the men. It should be women and children first, shouldn't it?'

'Rhys, are you sure you're OK? You're not infected?'

'Nah. Takes more than a bit of a sniffle to knock me down, love.' She heard him sneeze. 'Say, when are you coming home, then?'

'Soon,' she lied. 'I'm glad you're feeling OK. I've just got a few things to clear up first. It's mad here.'

'Sure, no worries. See you later. Take care!'

She closed the phone and bit her lip. She wanted to see him, to be sure that he wasn't infected, but she needed time in the Hub to recover. Just another half an hour, and then she would go home; get something to eat with Rhys, go to bed. She'd have to think up a suitable story about her hand. *No, I cut it on a piece of broken glass. Stupid, really. Serves me right.* That would have to do instead of *No, I had it sliced open while I was helping to save the world again, you know how it is…*

Walking down the steps leading to the Autopsy Room, Gwen could see Ianto on the lower level. He had an assortment of buckets, mops and detergents at his feet. He worked with a steady efficiency, his face impassive, unreadable. He was clean and back in his suit, but there were wounds inside, she knew that.

Owen followed her, hands in pockets. He looked as tired and hungry as she felt.

Jack came out of his office, pulling his braces into position over a fresh shirt. He'd washed and changed and the scars were already beginning to disappear. There might have been a distant, drawn look in the blue eyes as they surveyed the Hub,

248

checking on each of his team in turn and every workstation, but that was the only indication of the ordeal he had been through.

When he caught sight of her watching him, a great, white smile broke across his face. 'What you lookin' at?' he asked mockingly.

'I dunno,' she said. 'Label's fallen off.'

There was a quiet bleep from Toshiko's workstation and she swivelled around in her chair. 'Rift's back to normal.'

'You mean after all that there's nothing wrong with it?' Owen asked.

'No, I said it's back to normal.' Toshiko waved a hand across the displays. 'All chronon discharge has vanished.'

'No more sparks,' said Jack.

'Whatever was happening before, it must have been the result of the Strepto incursion,' Toshiko nodded. 'Saskia must have been trying to bring it all to a conclusion.'

'She did that all right,' said Owen.

'With a bit of help from us.'

Another alarm rang, and the Rift monitors flashed. Toshiko whirled in her seat. 'Uh oh. Energy spike in the Leckwith area. Something's coming through...'

Owen joined her. 'I recognise that energy signature. It's the Hokrala lawyers. They're sending another writ.'

'Let's go, everybody,' Jack said loudly, clapping his hands for attention. 'Welcoming party to the SUV now. Full kit. Let's go!'

He headed for the exit, grabbing his coat as he left, long strides carrying him to the cog-wheel door. He didn't even look back. He knew the others would be right behind him.

Also available from BBC Books

TORCHWOOD
ANOTHER LIFE
Peter Anghelides

ISBN 978 0 563 48653 4
UK £6.99 US$11.99/$14.99 CDN

Thick black clouds are blotting out the skies over Cardiff. As twenty-four inches of rain fall in twenty-four hours, the city centre's drainage system collapses. The capital's homeless are being murdered, their mutilated bodies left lying in the soaked streets around the Blaidd Drwg nuclear facility.

Tracked down by Torchwood, the killer calmly drops eight storeys to his death. But the killings don't stop. Their investigations lead Jack Harkness, Gwen Cooper and Toshiko Sato to a monster in a bathroom, a mystery at an army base and a hunt for stolen nuclear fuel rods. Meanwhile, Owen Harper goes missing from the Hub, when a game in *Second Reality* leads him to an old girlfriend...

Something is coming, forcing its way through the Rift, straight into Cardiff Bay.

Featuring Captain Jack Harkness as played by John Barrowman, with Gwen Cooper, Owen Harper, Toshiko Sato and Ianto Jones as played by Eve Myles, Burn Gorman, Naoki Mori and Gareth David-Lloyd, in the hit series created by Russell T Davies for BBC Television.

TORCHWOOD
BORDER PRINCES
Dan Abnett

ISBN 978 0 563 48654 1
UK £6.99 US$11.99/$14.99 CDN

The End of the World began on a Thursday night in October, just after eight in the evening…

The Amok is driving people out of their minds, turning them into zombies and causing riots in the streets. A solitary diner leaves a Cardiff restaurant, his mission to protect the Principal leading him to a secret base beneath a water tower. Everyone has a headache, there's something in Davey Morgan's shed, and the church of St Mary-in-the-Dust, demolished in 1840, has reappeared – though it's not due until 2011. Torchwood seem to be out of their depth. What will all this mean for the romance between Torchwood's newest members?

Captain Jack Harkness has something more to worry about: an alarm, an early warning, given to mankind and held – inert – by Torchwood for 108 years. And now it's flashing. Something is coming. Or something is already here.

Featuring Captain Jack Harkness as played by John Barrowman, with Gwen Cooper, Owen Harper, Toshiko Sato and Ianto Jones as played by Eve Myles, Burn Gorman, Naoki Mori and Gareth David-Lloyd, in the hit series created by Russell T Davies for BBC Television.

TORCHWOOD
SLOW DECAY
Andy Lane

ISBN 978 0 563 48655 8
UK £6.99 US$11.99/$14.99 CDN

When Torchwood track an energy surge to a Cardiff nightclub, the team finds the police are already at the scene. Five teenagers have died in a fight, and lying among the bodies is an unfamiliar device. Next morning, they discover the corpse of a Weevil, its face and neck eaten away, seemingly by human teeth. And on the streets of Cardiff, an ordinary woman with an extraordinary hunger is attacking people and eating her victims.

The job of a lifetime it might be, but working for Torchwood is putting big strains on Gwen's relationship with Rhys. While she decides to spice up their love life with the help of alien technology, Rhys decides it's time to sort himself out – better music, healthier food, lose some weight. Luckily, a friend has mentioned Doctor Scotus's weight-loss clinic…

Featuring Captain Jack Harkness as played by John Barrowman, with Gwen Cooper, Owen Harper, Toshiko Sato and Ianto Jones as played by Eve Myles, Burn Gorman, Naoki Mori and Gareth David-Lloyd, in the hit series created by Russell T Davies for BBC Television.

Also available from BBC Books

TORCHWOOD
TRACE MEMORY
David Llewellyn

ISBN 978 1 84607 438 7
UK £6.99 US$11.99/$14.99 CDN

Tiger Bay, Cardiff, 1953. A mysterious crate is brought into the docks on a Scandinavian cargo ship. Its destination: the Torchwood Institute. As the crate is offloaded by a group of local dockers, it explodes, killing all but one of them, a young Butetown lad called Michael Bellini.

Fifty-five years later, a radioactive source somewhere inside the Hub leads Torchwood to discover the same Michael Bellini, still young and dressed in his 1950s clothes, cowering in the vaults. They soon realise that each has encountered Michael before – as a child in Osaka, as a junior doctor, as a young police constable, as a new recruit to Torchwood One. But it's Jack who remembers him best of all.

Michael's involuntary time-travelling has something to do with a radiation-charged relic held inside the crate. And the Men in Bowler Hats are coming to get it back.

Featuring Captain Jack Harkness as played by John Barrowman, with Gwen Cooper, Owen Harper, Toshiko Sato and Ianto Jones as played by Eve Myles, Burn Gorman, Naoki Mori and Gareth David-Lloyd, in the hit series created by Russell T Davies for BBC Television.

Also available from BBC Books

T O R C H W O O D
THE TWILIGHT STREETS
Gary Russell

ISBN 978 1 84607 439 4
UK £6.99 US$11.99/$14.99 CDN

There's a part of the city that no one much goes to, a collection of rundown old houses and gloomy streets. No one stays there long, and no one can explain why – something's not quite right there.

Now the Council is renovating the district, and a new company is overseeing the work. There will be street parties and events to show off the newly gentrified neighbourhood: clowns and face-painters for the kids, magicians for the adults – the street entertainers of Cardiff, out in force.

None of this is Torchwood's problem. Until Toshiko recognises the sponsor of the street parties: Bilis Manger.

Now there is something for Torchwood to investigate. But Captain Jack Harkness has never been able to get into the area; it makes him physically ill to go near it. Without Jack's help, Torchwood must face the darker side of urban Cardiff alone…

Featuring Captain Jack Harkness as played by John Barrowman, with Gwen Cooper, Owen Harper, Toshiko Sato and Ianto Jones as played by Eve Myles, Burn Gorman, Naoki Mori and Gareth David-Lloyd, in the hit series created by Russell T Davies for BBC Television.